Love's Bloom

A Lilac Lake Book

By

Judith Keim

BOOKS BY JUDITH KEIM

THE HARTWELL WOMEN SERIES:
    The Talking Tree – 1
    Sweet Talk – 2
    Straight Talk – 3
    Baby Talk – 4
    The Hartwell Women – Boxed Set

THE BEACH HOUSE HOTEL SERIES:
    Breakfast at The Beach House Hotel – 1
    Lunch at The Beach House Hotel – 2
    Dinner at The Beach House Hotel – 3
    Christmas at The Beach House Hotel – 4
    Margaritas at The Beach House Hotel – 5
    Dessert at The Beach House Hotel – 6
    Coffee at The Beach House Hotel – 7
    High Tea at The Beach House Hotel – 8
    Nightcaps at The Beach House Hotel – 9
    Bubbles at The Beach House Hotel – 10
    Canapes at The Beach House Hotel – 11 (2025)

THE FAT FRIDAYS GROUP:
    Fat Fridays – 1
    Sassy Saturdays – 2
    Secret Sundays – 3

THE SALTY KEY INN SERIES:
    Finding Me – 1
    Finding My Way – 2
    Finding Love – 3
    Finding Family – 4
    The Salty Key Inn Series – Boxed Set

SEASHELL COTTAGE BOOKS:

A Christmas Star

Change of Heart

A Summer of Surprises

A Road Trip to Remember

The Beach Babes

THE CHANDLER HILL INN SERIES:

Going Home – 1

Coming Home – 2

Home at Last – 3

The Chandler Hill Inn Series – Boxed Set

THE DESERT SAGE INN SERIES:

The Desert Flowers – Rose – 1

The Desert Flowers – Lily – 2

The Desert Flowers – Willow – 3

The Desert Flowers – Mistletoe & Holly – 4

The Desert Sage Inn Series – Boxed Set

SOUL SISTERS AT CEDAR MOUNTAIN LODGE:

Christmas Sisters – Anthology

Christmas Kisses

Christmas Castles

Christmas Stories – Soul Sisters Anthology

Christmas Joy

The Christmas Joy Boxed Set

THE SANDERLING COVE INN SERIES:

Waves of Hope – 1

Sandy Wishes – 2

Salty Kisses – 3

THE LILAC LAKE INN SERIES

Love by Design – 1

Love Between the Lines – 2

Love Under the Stars – 3

LILAC LAKE BOOKS

Love's Cure

Love's Home Run

Love's Bloom – (2025)

Love's Harvest – (2025)

Love's Match – (2026)

OTHER BOOKS:

The ABCs of Living With a Dachshund

Winning BIG – a little love story for all ages

Holiday Hopes

The Winning Tickets

For more information: **www.judithkeim.com**

PRAISE FOR JUDITH KEIM'S NOVELS

THE BEACH HOUSE HOTEL SERIES – Books 1 – 10:

"Love the characters in this series. This series was my first introduction to Judith Keim. She is now one of my favorites. Looking forward to reading more of her books."

BREAKFAST AT THE BEACH HOUSE HOTEL – *"An easy, delightful read that offers romance, family relationships, and strong women learning to be stronger. Real life situations filter through the pages. Enjoy!"*

LUNCH AT THE BEACH HOUSE HOTEL – *"This series is such a joy to read. You feel you are actually living with them. Can't wait to read the latest one."*

DINNER AT THE BEACH HOUSE HOTEL – *"A Terrific Read! As usual, Judith Keim did it again. Enjoyed immensely. Continue writing such pleasantly reading books for all of us readers."*

CHRISTMAS AT THE BEACH HOUSE HOTEL – *"Not Just Another Christmas Novel. This is book number four in the series and my introduction to Judith Keim's writing. I wasn't disappointed. The characters are dimensional and engaging. The plot is well crafted and advances at a pleasing pace.*

MARGARITAS AT THE BEACH HOUSE HOTEL – *"Overall, Margaritas at the Beach House Hotel is another wonderful addition to the series. Judith Keim takes the reader on a journey told through the voices of these amazing characters we have all come to love through the years!*

DESSERT AT THE BEACH HOUSE HOTEL – *"It is a heartwarming and beautiful women's fiction as only Judith Keim can do with her wonderful characters, amazing location. and family and friends whose daily lives circle around Ann and Rhonda and The Beach House Hotel.*

COFFEE AT THE BEACH HOUSE HOTEL – *"Great story and characters! A hard to put down book. Lots of things happening, including a kidnapping of a young boy. The Beach House Hotel is a wonderful hotel run by two women who are best friends. Highly recommend this book.*

HIGH TEA AT THE BEACH HOUSE HOTEL – *"What a lovely story! The Beach House Hotel series is a always a great read. Each book in the series brings a new aspect to the saga of Ann and Rhonda."*

THE HARTWELL WOMEN SERIES – Books 1 – 4:

"This was an EXCELLENT series. When I discovered Judith Keim, I read all of her books back to back. I thoroughly enjoyed the women Keim has written about. They are believable and you want to just jump into their lives and be their friends! I can't wait for any upcoming books!"

"I fell into Judith Keim's Hartwell Women series and have read & enjoyed all of her books in every series. Each centers around a strong & interesting woman character and their family interaction. Good reads that leave you wanting more."

THE FAT FRIDAYS GROUP – Books 1 – 3:

"Excellent story line for each character, and an insightful representation of situations which deal with some of the contemporary issues women are faced with today."

THE SALTY KEY INN SERIES – Books 1 – 4:

FINDING ME – *"The characters are endearing with the same struggles we all encounter. The setting makes me feel like I am a guest at The Salty Key Inn...relaxed, happy & light-hearted! The men are yummy and the women strong. You can't get better than that! Happy Reading!"*

FINDING MY WAY - *"Loved the family dynamics as well as uncertain emotions of dating and falling in love. Appreciated the morals and strength of parenting throughout. Just couldn't put this book down."*

FINDING LOVE – *"Judith Keim always puts substance into her books. This book was no different, I learned about PTSD, accepting oneself, there are always going to be problems but stick it out and make it work.*

FINDING FAMILY – *"Completing this series is like eating the last chip. Love Judith's writing and her female characters are always smart, strong, vulnerable to life and love experiences."*

"This was a refreshing book. Bringing the heart and soul of the family to us."

THE CHANDLER HILL INN SERIES – Books 1 – 3:

GOING HOME – *"I was completely immersed in this book, with the beautiful descriptive writing, and the author's way of bringing her characters to life. I felt like I was right inside her story."*

COMING HOME – *"Coming Home was such a wonderful story. The author has such a gift for getting the reader right to the heart of things."*

HOME AT LAST – *"In this wonderful conclusion, to a heartfelt and emotional trilogy set in Oregon's stunning wine country, Judith Keim has tied up the Chandler Hill series with the perfect bow."*

SEASHELL COTTAGE BOOKS:

A CHRISTMAS STAR – "Love, laughter, sadness, great food, and hope for the future, all in one book. It doesn't get any better than this stunning read."

CHANGE OF HEART – "CHANGE OF HEART is the summer read we've all been waiting for. Judith Keim is a master at creating fascinating characters that are simply irresistible. Her stories leave you with a big smile on your face and a heart bursting with love."
~Kellie Coates Gilbert, author of the popular Sun Valley Series

A SUMMER OF SURPRISES – "Ms. Keim uses this book as an amazing platform to show that with hard emotional work, belief in yourself, and love, the scars of abuse can be conquered. It in no way preaches, it's a lovely story with a happy ending."

A ROAD TRIP TO REMEMBER – "The characters are so real that they jump off the page. Such a fun, HAPPY book at the perfect time. It will lift your spirits and even remind you of your own grandmother. Spirited and hopeful Aggie gets a second chance at love and she takes the steering wheel and drives straight for it."

THE BEACH BABES – "Another winner at the pen of Judith Keim. I love the characters and the book just flows. It feels as though you are at the beach with them and are a part of you.

THE DESERT SAGE INN SERIES – Books 1 – 4:

THE DESERT FLOWERS – ROSE – "The Desert Flowers - Rose, "In this first of a series, we see each woman come into her own and view new beginnings even as they must take this tearful journey as they slowly lose a dear friend.

THE DESERT FLOWERS – LILY – *"The second book in the Desert Flowers series is just as wonderful as the first. Judith Keim is a brilliant storyteller. Her characters are truly lovely and people that you want to be friends with as soon as you start reading. Judith Keim is not afraid to weave real-life conflict and loss into her stories.*

THE DESERT FLOWERS – WILLOW – *"The feelings of love, joy, happiness, friendship, family, and the pain of loss are deeply felt by Willow Sanchez and her two cohorts Rose and Lily. The Desert Flowers met because of their deep feelings for Alec Thurston, a man who touched their lives in different ways."*

MISTLETOE AND HOLLY – *"As always, the author never ceases to amaze me. She's able to take characters and bring them to life in such a way that you think you're actually among family. It's a great holiday read. You won't be disappointed."*

THE SANDERLING COVE INN SERIES – Books 1 – 3:

WAVES OF HOPE – *"Such a wonderful story about several families in a beautiful location in Florida. A grandmother requests her three granddaughters to help her by running the family's inn for the summer. Other grandmothers in the area played a part in this plan to find happiness for their grandsons and granddaughters."*

SANDY WISHES – *"Three cousins needing a change and a few of the neighborhood boys from when they were young are back visiting their grandmothers. It is an adventure, a summer of discoveries, and embracing the person they are becoming."*

SALTY KISSES – *"I love this story, as well as the entire series because it's about family, friendship, and love. The meddling grandmothers have only the best intentions and want to see their grandchildren find love and happiness. What grandparent wouldn't want that?"*

THE LILAC LAKE INN SERIES – Books 1 – 3:

LOVE BY DESIGN –"*Genie Wittner is planning on selling her beloved Lilac Inn B&B, and keeping a cottage for her three granddaughters, Whitney, the movie star, Dani an architect, and Taylor a writer. A little mystery, a possible ghost, and romance all make this a great read and the start of a new series.*"

LOVE BETWEEN THE LINES – "*Taylor is one of 3 sisters who have inherited a cottage in Lilac Lake from their grandmother. She is an accomplished author who is having some issues getting inspired for her next book. Things only get worse when she receives an email from her new editor with a harsh critique of her last book. She's still fuming when Cooper shows up in town, determined to work together on getting the book ready.*"

LOVE UNDER THE STARS – "*Love Under the Stars is the third book in The Lilac Lake Inn Series by author Judith Keim. Judith beautifully weaves together the final story in this amazing series about the Gilford sisters and their grandmother, GG.*"

THE LILAC LAKE BOOKS

LOVE'S CURE – *Welcome back to Lilac Lake with a new spin-off series from author Judith Keim. For fans of the author, you will be reunited with previous characters, as well as being introduced to new ones. Even though this book can be read as a stand-alone, I highly recommend reading the Lilac Lake Inn series to get introduced to all of these amazing characters.*

Love's Bloom

A Lilac Lake Book

By

Judith Keim

Wild Quail Publishing

Dedication

For all my gardening readers...

May your lives bloom with love and happiness.

CHAPTER ONE

MISTY OWENS SAT WITH SEVERAL FRIENDS AT THE TABLE usually reserved for locals in Jake's Bar and Grill on Main Street in Lilac Lake, New Hampshire. She was pleased to have their company. Since moving back to her small hometown following a disastrous relationship with an emotionally and physically abusive man who still troubled her dreams, she needed to feel connected to good people who truly cared about one another.

Of all the men who sat at the table that evening, she was attracted to David Graham, who owned a successful landscaping business with his father. Gentle, kind, and handsome, he was everything she wanted in a man if only she could get through her past issues.

She warmed under David's friendly smile and knew he was interested in her. But how would she ever be able to explain to him what had gone on in the past and how it had affected her? Many in town had seen her bruises and heard her tale of running away from her apartment in Florida to the safety of her home. But not many knew she still struggled with the aftermath of Vince Tucci's abuse of her. That issue would take time to get over, as would learning to trust a man again.

As Misty munched on her chicken Caesar salad, she studied the men and women sitting around her and listened as they caught up with one another's daily activities. She glanced at her sister, Crystal, who'd recently sold the Lilac Lake Café to a couple of Melissa Hendrickson's friends from Boston. As the town was growing and members of their group were pairing off, many changes were taking place.

Tomorrow, she'd move into the cabin she'd rented by the river flowing outside of town. It was the beginning of a whole new life. A happy one, she hoped.

The next morning, Misty sat on the living room couch in the cabin and stared at the pile of boxes in the middle of the room. David and his friend, Aaron Collister, had moved the furniture and heavy items into the one-bedroom cabin. Now, all she had to do was unpack the boxes.
She leaned back against the couch cushions and sighed. This change was very important. In part, it meant having independence from her big sister. Crystal had always taken care of her because their mother was an alcoholic and addict who couldn't. Now, Misty needed to stand on her own.

Misty was both scared and excited to be alone. She'd spent a few years teaching school in Florida before she'd escaped and returned to New Hampshire to stay with Crystal, who was nine years older.

Shaking off the memory of that frantic drive home, Misty

got up and went to the sliding glass door leading outside, opened it, and stepped onto the wooden deck overlooking the river. She loved living in one of the small, upscale cabins scattered in the woods along the riverbank. Being outdoors among nature had always been soothing to her. Even as a child, she often played quietly by the river or enjoyed activities with others on Lilac Lake.

Though their childhood had been difficult, the residents of their small town did what they could to help Misty and Crystal through the trauma of their lives. While Crystal could remember when their mother wasn't stoned, drugged, or drunk, by the time Misty became aware of such things, that's all she saw of her mother.

Leaning over the deck railing, Misty listened to the song of a cardinal, saw a flash of red wings, and grinned. Cardinals were lucky for her. She hoped this bird had plenty of it to share. With this new chapter of her life, she was going to need it.

She went inside and studied the compact space whose white walls sparkled from care. This home was a lucky find for her. She and a new teacher friend, Hazel Belmont, had rented the last two available cabins. They'd already planned to save gas by taking turns driving to the local elementary school.

Misty had just opened a box and was staring at the lamps inside when David appeared carrying a large potted plant and a bouquet of mixed summer flowers.

"Thought you could use these," he said. "It's a healthy sign to have live greenery around. Something about Feng Shui."

"They're both gorgeous! I love them," said Misty. "Thanks so much. Did these come from your company?"

David grinned and nodded. Graham Landscaping was a big operation in town. The business had doubled in size when David returned to town after earning his degree from Cornell University's College of Agriculture and Life Sciences.

The company now had maintenance contracts in both winter and summer for most of the businesses in the area. The Woodlands, an assisted-living complex outside of town, and The Meadows, a new, upscale housing development owned by Brad and Aaron Collister at the end of the lake, had both retained Graham Landscaping for their services.

"Where do you want the plant?" David asked. "Maybe over there by the sliding door?"

"Perfect," said Misty, hurrying to make space for it.

David handed her the flowers and then set the plant down.

Misty stared at the mixture of red and orange roses, yellow zinnias, and field flowers she couldn't name. "These are beautiful."

"I thought you might like them," said David. His deep-blue gaze focused on her as he swept a lock of brown, sun-streaked hair off his brow. "I know this move is important to you, and I want it to be a positive experience."

She returned his smile. "Thanks again. I'm glad we're friends. You and Aaron did a great job of helping me move into this cabin. I couldn't have done it without you. How can I ever repay you?"

"Just be safe here and enjoy this spot," David said. "I've got to go back to work. See you later."

"Thanks," she said, walking him to the front door.

After he left, she put the flowers in a pitcher of water and wrapped her arms around herself. David was very special.

She was busy unpacking boxes in the kitchen when Crystal dropped in, carrying a carton. "I think I have this by mistake. It looks like books you might use in your classroom."

With the sale of the Lilac Lake Café, both Misty and Crystal were moving out of the apartment above it.

Misty motioned for Crystal to set the box down on the counter. "Thanks. I would've eventually realized it was missing."

"How are you doing with your share of our move?" Misty asked Crystal.

"Good, I guess," Crystal replied. "I never realized how much stuff I have."

They laughed together, remembering how easy they'd thought it would be.

Love and gratitude filled Misty as she smiled at Crystal, the sister she adored. Crystal was a blond beauty with lavender/blue eyes that matched the purple hair she'd dyed recently. Now, only a soft streak of purple remained.

Misty had always wanted to look like Crystal, but her tan skin, dark eyes, and straight black hair were no match. As a teen, she'd dyed her hair blond, but after several years, she'd allowed her natural dark color to return. Now, when people told her how pretty she was, Misty accepted it as the compliment it was meant to be.

"Where'd you get the flowers?" Crystal asked her.

"David Graham brought them, along with the plant, standing by the sliding glass door."

"He's such a sweet, interesting man," said Crystal. "Just before you moved back to Lilac Lake, his sister died after a long struggle with cancer. The family was heartbroken. David initiated a fundraiser to buy an empty lot in town so they could create a small, tranquil garden and park in her memory. It's become a coveted spot where people can sit on a bench, enjoy the flower beds, and take a break."

"I've seen it from a distance as I drove by but have never taken the time to stop," said Misty. "Next time I'm on that street, I'll spend some time there."

"Didn't David also help you move in here?" Crystal said.

"He and Aaron," Misty said. "Why?"

"Aaron's another great guy," said Crystal. "I love this town and how everyone is willing to offer help and support to others. Thank God. That's what got both of us to this moment in time."

"I remember how people rallied around us when we were growing up," she said.

"And how they supported my work at the Café," Crystal added. "I have them to thank for making such a healthy profit with its sale."

"I'm proud of what you accomplished," said Misty. "But then, you've always been the strong one."

Crystal hugged her. "No, Misty. You're the resilient one. You've gone through so much. I hope, now that you're on your own again, you'll find the happiness you deserve. And remember, you may be living alone, but your friends and I are here to help you."

Warmth flooded through her. Misty squeezed her sister with affection. "I know that. Thanks."

Crystal looked around. "This is such an adorable place. I love that in addition to the master bedroom suite, you have a small office, a big kitchen, and a fireplace in the living area for those cold winter days."

"It's ideal for me," said Misty. "Hazel and I were able to get the last two renovated cabins. I like her and think we're going to be close friends." From the South, Hazel and her pronounced southern drawl enchanted everyone.

"I like her too," said Crystal. She checked her watch. "I'd better get back to work at Emmett's house. We're trying to make room for my things yet keep the décor to what we both like."

"Are you going to be sad to stop working permanently at the Café, helping out the new owners and being out of the apartment?"

Crystal thought for a moment. "It's going to feel strange. That's for sure. But I think the plan to work with Melissa on special events like gourmet dinners will be interesting."

Melissa Hendrickson's family's restaurant, Fins, had been destroyed by fire, and though Melissa didn't want to give up professional cooking entirely, she was thinking of doing some projects with Crystal.

"Something will work out," said Misty. "Just like you've always told me."

Crystal's lips curved. "It'll work out for you, too."

After Crystal left, Misty went back to unpacking. She left the box of books for the last project, thinking she'd take them into the elementary school when she went to set up her classroom.

Misty grabbed a bottle of water from the refrigerator and took some time to go through the books she'd kept on a shelf in her Florida classroom so that whenever a student had time to read, they were there.

She lifted a favorite book of hers and opened it. She let out a loud shriek and dropped it on the counter. Someone had written "**FUCK YOU**" in bold letters across the first page.

It took a moment for Misty to catch her breath.

Her mind raced.

She knew who'd written those nasty words. Her ex-boyfriend. Tears blurred her vision as she picked up her beloved book with two fingers and dropped it into the box holding the trash. Vince Tucci was such a pig.

Thinking of him, Misty felt a shiver run across her

shoulders. She hurried outside onto the deck, where she could inhale fresh air and feel the sun's warmth. She'd told her sister about most of what had happened. But even with the help of a therapist, she couldn't describe the feeling of being treated worse than an unwanted animal. Angry, taunting words and sneers hurt worse than the punches. When she'd gathered her strength, she'd sneaked out of her apartment in the middle of the night and come home to Lilac Lake, where she felt safe.

She was still standing on the deck when she heard someone come into the house. She whipped around and then relaxed when she saw it was Whitney Gilford Woodruff carrying a basket.

Misty went inside to greet her. Whitney was, at one time, a famous actress who'd given up that life to live in Lilac Lake, a beloved summer retreat for her while growing up.

"I've brought a basket of goodies to help stock your pantry and add to your refrigerator," said Whitney cheerfully as she walked into the kitchen. "I know Melissa is making dinner for you, and Crystal, Dani, and Taylor are doing other things." She stopped talking and studied her. "What's wrong?"

Misty pointed to the box of rubbish. "In there. Check out the book."

Whitney lifted the book out of the box and placed it on the counter. "What am I looking for?"

"Just open it. You'll see," said Misty.

Whitney did as she was told and jumped at seeing the scrawled words. "My word! Who did that?"

"My old boyfriend, the bastard," said Misty, clutching her hands.

Whitney frowned. "Has he come around here recently?"

"No. That was done in the past. I didn't see it until today."

Whitney hugged her. "Crystal made sure that Nick was aware of your past, and she asked him to keep an eye out for your ex-boyfriend. If you don't mind, I will tell him about this and ask him to remind his staff to be alert to seeing or hearing about strangers asking for you."

"That would be great," said Misty. "The last I heard, Vince was living with his new girlfriend." She eagerly changed the subject. "Let's see what's in your basket."

"A little bit of everything." Whitney showed Misty the three cheeses she'd brought, several kinds of crackers and cookies, olives, a small box of chocolates from Petals, pear jam, and a marinade for chicken.

"This is like Christmas," gushed Misty, touched. "I've got the basics, but this is a whole lot more fun."

"I'm glad you like it. Is there anything I can do for you?"

Misty shook her head. "I'm just taking care of the last details, and that is something I need to do myself. But thanks."

"Okay, then, I'll see you later. You know who to call if you ever need help with your ex. Even though he's my husband, I say Nick's the best chief of police Lilac Lake has ever had."

"Yes, he is. We all know that. He's been superb."

The two women hugged goodbye, and feeling better, Misty went into her bedroom to make the bed. She'd bought a new bedspread and two new pillows, and she couldn't wait to see what it looked like.

A short while later, she stood back to assess the queen-size bed and admired the linen quilted spread in a soft gray that was lighter than the dark gray walls. Sitting between the two white pillows was the brown teddy bear that had been a huge comfort to her through the years. Tattered and mended, she kept it as a reminder of how far she'd come in her life. Crystal had wrapped it up for her one Christmas, telling her it was from their mother, which Misty knew wasn't true. It was the thought behind it that made the bear special, proving the loving connection she had with her sister.

She heard someone at the door and, after opening it, found Melissa holding a couple of insulated food carriers.

"Hi, I hope you're hungry," said Melissa. "I got carried away, but then I thought this would be enough food to carry you through a couple of days."

"Thank you." Misty ushered her into the kitchen.

After Melissa had set the carrier down on the counter, Misty hugged her. "It sure smells delicious, whatever it is."

Melissa unzipped the bag. "I've made my favorite lemon chicken casserole, fresh tomato spaghetti sauce, a green bean salad, cold chicken salad, fresh boiled shrimp with cocktail sauce, and my special salad dressing. I've put in fresh, clean lettuce and pasta for you to use."

Misty chuckled. "Thanks. I guess you miss cooking in the restaurant, huh?"

Melissa gave her a sheepish grin. "Yes and no. I'm happy to do this for you."

As Melissa and Misty talked, Whitney's sisters, Dani and Taylor, arrived.

"I've brought wine, enough for us to share now if you wish," said Dani.

"And I brought appetizers for today and later," Taylor said.

"Okay," said Misty. "I unpacked wine glasses. Let's use them. And thank you, everyone, for such a nice housewarming."

She opened a bottle of chardonnay and poured the white wine into four separate glasses. "I've got four chairs on the deck. Let's go outside."

The women carried their wine glasses and a tray of appetizers out onto the deck and formed a comfortable circle.

"It's so pretty here," said Taylor.

"Here's to a wonderful life in your new home," Dani said, lifting her glass.

They clicked glasses with one another and took sips.

Misty looked around at her friends and fought tears for the second time that day.

CHAPTER TWO

AFTER THE WOMEN LEFT TO GO HOME TO THEIR FAMILIES, Misty locked the front door. She'd already made sure that the double lock on the sliding glass door was in place, and she knew the windows throughout the cabin were locked. Once she got used to the sounds in and around the house, she'd relax a little more. But for now, this made her feel safe.

Misty was happy to be on her own again but knew it would take some adjustment. If only she hadn't seen that ugly scrawl of words. She couldn't get an image of Vince's handsome, beguiling, awful face out of her mind.

Dusk was easing in, changing the blue sky to gray. Misty knew that she'd feel much better once she made it through the night.

She called Hazel and was forced to leave a message: "Sorry, I won't be able to come to your house tonight. I'm exhausted and will catch up with you tomorrow."

After seeing that the kitchen was cleaned up, a habit from living with Crystal, Misty padded into her new, luxurious bathroom and got ready for bed.

A few minutes later, she climbed beneath the sheets, curled up with her pillow, and finally slept.

###

Misty stirred and opened her eyes to find a rosy dawn emerging outside her bedroom window overlooking the river. Feeling as if she'd run a marathon during the night, she got out of bed and decided to walk into town. She needed exercise and time away from the cabin to chill out from the horrible dreams that had kept her tossing and turning.

She pulled on a pair of shorts and a T-shirt, got into her walking shoes, and left the house, determined to have a nice day.

Birds were singing and flitting about in the trees above her as she left the river and walked to the corner of Main Street to head downtown. On a whim, she walked one block over to see if she could find the special little garden park dedicated to David's sister.

On the way, Misty chided herself for allowing memories of Vince to ruin the new life she was building in Lilac Lake. She realized if she didn't move forward, she'd be trapped forever in a circle of regrets and self-recriminations. She remembered the state motto of New Hampshire—"Live Free or Die"—and knew she needed to let the past go. It was over, and she would find a way to cope. Lord knew she'd learned to pretend things were all right when they weren't.

She'd walked a couple of blocks when she saw the park.

As she got closer, she noticed someone kneeling by the flower beds and realized it was David. She approached him.

"Good morning! You're here early."

He looked up at her and grinned, then got to his feet. "This is a nice time of day to do some weeding and make sure everything looks fine."

"My sister told me about the park, and I wanted to see it for myself. What you're doing is a labor of love."

He stared into the distance. "My sister, Lily, and I were very close, like you and Crystal. Growing up, I was small until I hit a big growth spurt. But until then, I was picked on enough that she kept an eye out for me and convinced me to take karate lessons. Now, I teach classes on it. But I'll never forget her loyalty."

Misty looked around. Edging the square of land, flower beds added color to the green grass at the center. Park benches were set in several locations, far enough apart to give privacy to those using them. A large maple tree sat along the back of the lot spreading its branches and providing shade over a portion of the park. A yellow brick walkway wound its way through the lot to the benches.

"I love the yellow brick 'road,'" Misty said. "It's like *The Wizard of Oz.*"

David let out a sigh. " '*Over the Rainbow*' was one of Lily's favorite songs. We listened to it together after she got sick." His voice was full of pain.

Misty reached out and touched his arm. "I'm sorry. I can't imagine what it must have been like for you to lose your sister."

"Doing this garden for her has been healing. The town's

support has meant a lot to me and my parents." He motioned for her to take a seat. "Go ahead and enjoy it. I won't disturb you. I'm almost done weeding."

Misty walked along the brick walkway to a bench in the back corner and sat down. Closing her eyes, she inhaled the smell of roses and other flowers, listened to the birds chirping in the maple tree, and felt a deep sense of peace wash over her. Her entire body relaxed, Misty vowed once more to refuse to allow anyone to take this feeling away from her.

"Misty?"

She looked up to see David walking toward her. She smiled and patted the empty space beside her. "This is so peaceful."

He slid onto the bench beside her. "That's what we were hoping for. It's a lot of work but worth it."

They sat quietly for a few minutes, and then David got to his feet. "Will you be at Jake's tonight?"

"Yes," said Misty. "I'm going to take advantage of meeting my friends there as much as possible before school starts."

"I'll see you later." David gave her a little salute.

She watched him go. He might've been small as a child, but he was tall now, with a muscular body toned handsomely by his work. She liked that he didn't gain muscle by constantly working out at a gym. That would remind her too much of Vince.

Misty continued her walk into town to the Lilac Lake Café. Though she and Crystal had moved out of the apartment above it, Crystal was temporarily helping at the café until

Nettie Mancini and her fiancé, Jason Rockwell, were comfortable enough with the operation to go forward without Crystal's help.

She arrived at the café just before six-thirty and waited with others for the door to open. Early morning hours were a reality in running the café, something Misty was delighted to avoid going forward.

She stood a moment and gazed at the town she loved so much. Bright-colored awnings covered some of the windows of the shops along Main Street. Matched by pots sitting by doorways and overflowing with summer flowers, it looked postcard-picture perfect as the small New England town it was.

After unlocking the door, Crystal and Nettie greeted the small gathering. Nettie had short, dark, curly hair, blue eyes, and a smile no one could resist. Though she wasn't tall, her body had an appealing curviness. Misty was thrilled that she'd be taking over the café. Jason, her fiancé, was just as nice and as eager as Nettie to make friends.

"Hi, Misty," said Nettie. "I heard you've moved into your new place."

"Moved is the operative word. Settled is another. But I'm getting there," said Misty. "When do you begin painting the apartment?"

"Not for a couple of days. Jason has a friend who's going to do it for us. His name is Vinnie."

Misty's heart jerked to a stop before her pulse began

pounding in her ears. "What's his full name?"

Nettie frowned. "Vinnie Morelli. Why?'

Misty sighed and shook her head. "Someone I knew was named Vince. Not a nice man."

"Oh, I get it. This Vinnie is a great guy who's worked for us for a couple of years. We're trying to get him interested in moving to Lilac Lake so he can work with us here."

"I'm sure he'll love it," said Misty, feeling her knees gain strength. In the last day, there'd been too many reminders of Vince. She went over to the counter and sat, needing a cup of coffee, her favorite, a mocha decaf. She glanced into the display case and ordered a maple raisin scone. In maple sugar country, lots of treats contained it.

Crystal stood by her seat. "Are you okay? Whitney told me about one of your books being ruined. Vince, no doubt?"

"I'm sure of it," said Misty. A shudder slithered snakelike across her shoulders.

"Whitney promised me that Nick was aware of it and that he'd talk to all his deputies about the situation." Crystal shook her head with dismay. "Thank goodness you got away from that jerk."

"A lesson learned," said Misty, setting her jaw in a firm line.

"Don't let that terrible experience ruin you for other relationships," said Crystal quietly before turning to seat more customers. "I see how David looks at you."

Misty sipped her coffee and took a bite of the warm scone. No wonder customers loved the Lilac Lake Café.

That evening, Misty and Hazel headed to Jake's.

The bar was busy and looked like most sports bars, with an array of televisions blaring a variety of games. Crystal waved to them from the large "locals" table at one corner of the room.

"Hi, y'all," said Hazel, settling in an empty chair beside Misty. Wearing blue jeans that clung to her long legs and a white T-shirt, she looked stunning. Her brown hair was pulled back in a ponytail, and her dark brown eyes sparkled. From a wealthy family, Hazel liked to downplay her appearance. But with her natural beauty, it worked in the opposite way.

From the other side of the table, David caught Misty's eye. She returned his smile, happy to see him.

By the time Melissa arrived with her fiancé, Ross Roberts, a former professional baseball player, there were sixteen people crowded around two large tables. Misty listened as Dani talked about the new cottages The Meadows would build along a section of lakefront property. Taylor shared news of a book she was writing, and others, including Dirk McArthur, the new young dentist in town, talked about what they were doing in their jobs. As they spoke, Misty realized how intertwined their lives were.

When Crystal told them she and Emmett were thinking seriously about eloping, Misty clapped with the others. Emmett's family situation was proving to be more and more awkward between his father, a U.S. Senator running for President, and his mother, who was recovering from alcohol addiction.

"The one reason I hesitate is that I want all of you to be part of the celebration," said Crystal.

"Just invite us to a party afterward," said Dani. "We definitely want to celebrate with you."

"I'll help you with that," Nettie said.

Crystal looked at Emmett, and they both smiled.

Though she was unsettled, Misty was delighted to see how happy her sister was.

At home, Misty walked through the rooms, making sure everything was all right, and then she headed to bed. Tomorrow, she and Hazel would go through the rest of the books in the box, hoping no others had become tainted by Vince's crude words. Misty supposed she could do the task herself, but when Hazel suggested she help, Misty couldn't turn down the offer.

She lay in bed, staring up at the ceiling. David's image came to her. She hoped they could become even better friends. Though she wasn't sure she was ready for anything more, the thought of a deeper friendship with him was intriguing.

When she awoke, Misty lay in bed listening to birds making music in the trees outside, and a smile tugged at her lips. This was the first day of the rest of her life, and it was going to be different from what she'd known. She could feel it in her bones.

She looked forward to her early morning walk to what she thought of as "David's Park" and decided to do it again. There was something special about sitting there. Maybe because David and his family had created the park with such love.

Misty got up and dressed for her walk. If she were lucky, David would be there.

After preparing for the day, Misty headed out.

As she looked up at the sky, she saw storm clouds gathering on the horizon and wondered if the weatherman was right and it would become a rainy day. The idea didn't depress her. They needed the rain, and a cozy day indoors would be peaceful.

Moving quickly, Misty soon arrived at the park. She scanned the area, but David wasn't there. Disappointed, she sat on one of the benches and looked out at the flowers. Each bed held different varieties of flowers, yet they all complemented one another.

While she was sitting on one of the back benches, she observed an auburn-haired woman walk into the park, go over to one of the rosebushes, and lean down to sniff one of its yellow buds.

The woman bowed her head and spoke softly before moving to a nearby bench.

"Lovely, isn't it," said Misty as she walked by the woman on her way out of the park.

The woman said, "Very special."

Out on the sidewalk, Misty looked back and noticed the woman had moved to the bench where she'd been sitting.

Misty couldn't help but wonder about her. She'd seemed so sad.

Misty walked into town and went to the Lilac Lake Café for her morning coffee.

Nettie greeted her at the door. "Another day of settling in?"

Misty let out a weary sigh. "I'm loving the space. I feel like I'm living in the woods and love all the activities of the birds there."

"Thanks again for your willingness to move out of the apartment quickly," said Nettie. "Jason and I can't wait to move in. Come in. The coffee is on me."

Misty saw Taylor writing at a table in the corner, waved, and then stood at the counter, waiting for her coffee. She was intent on getting back to the cabin to finish getting established in her home.

On the walk back home, she enjoyed the sights and sounds of the townspeople preparing for another summer day. Shopkeepers were opening, watering pots of flowers outside their doors or mounting American flags next to their entrances. It was like the setting of a Hallmark movie. She loved it. When she was back at school, she wouldn't be able to take advantage of early morning walks like this, and she wanted to treasure each one.

Hazel and she were excited to be working at the same school. Though they were very different and from extremely different backgrounds, they got along well. It was important to Misty to foster the friendship of someone more her age than her sister's.

When she got to her small riverside neighborhood, Misty stood for a moment, looking at the cabins. Some of the larger original ones had log exteriors. Hers, a smaller, newer cabin, had a gray clapboard exterior. All of them, she knew, were modern and up-to-date inside.

JoEllen Daniels appeared from a cabin a distance from hers, climbed into her car, and drove away. Having JoEllen as a neighbor was the only drawback to the neighborhood. JoEllen was a woman desperate to find a man and would do anything to get her way.

She glanced at Hazel's cabin, two doors down from hers. All was quiet.

Misty unlocked her front door and entered the house. She could see most of her space from the entrance with one glance. Her gaze rested on the plant by the sliding glass door, and she was touched once more by David's gesture.

She walked into the kitchen and stared at the box on the floor. How in the world had Vince managed to write inside one of the books? She must have said or done something to set him off. But then, she never knew what would make him angry.

Misty sighed and made a list of the groceries and other items she needed for the cabin. Crystal had given her furniture, dishes, and some kitchenware from the apartment.

Misty had also kept some things that had been shipped to her from the apartment she'd shared with another woman in Florida. But now, she wanted a fresh look. A trip to Target in Concord might be in order.

She'd finished making her bed when she heard someone at the front door. She went to answer it and found Hazel standing there. "Hi, come in," Misty said. "Can I get you a cup of coffee or tea?'

"Coffee would be lovely," said Hazel, sounding like a refined Southern lady.

Hazel followed her into the kitchen and glanced around. "You've done a wonderful job of getting unpacked and settled."

"I'm going to Concord to pick up some extra things I need. Want to come?" Misty asked, handing Hazel a cup of coffee with a dash of cream like she usually had.

"Sure," said Hazel. "I can use some decorative items. I'm glad we found these cabins. They're fabulous."

"It's a great location," said Misty. She stared at the box she dreaded to go through.

Hazel noticed and set down her coffee cup. "We might as well do it."

"Okay." Misty knelt on the floor next to the box and handed the books to Hazel, who checked to make sure they were clear of any writing.

They were down to the last two when Hazel said, "Here's one." She held up the book to show her. "CUNT" was written there.

Feeling sick to her stomach, Misty said, "Please put it in the rubbish box over there." She pointed to a large cardboard box filled with paper and trash.

"Okay, last one," said Hazel, her voice shaking. "Who in the world would do this kind of thing?" She opened the book. "This one is clear."

Misty heaved a sigh of relief and got to her feet. "I'm glad that's over. Thank you, Hazel. I didn't want to be alone to do this. It's so creepy it makes my skin crawl."

"Yeah, he's one sick dude," said Hazel.

"I know it can't be anyone else because I had to remove books from my classroom so they could paint the room. They were sitting in a box in my apartment. We got into a fight, and he dumped the books out of the box onto the floor. He must've gone back and written in a couple of them before I boxed them up again."

Hazel gave her an encouraging look. "Let's forget about him and go shopping. I'm feeling creative."

Misty's tension disappeared, relieved the drama was over.

CHAPTER THREE

LATER THAT DAY, MISTY LOOKED AT HER PURCHASES with satisfaction. Each additional decorative touch made the space inside the cabin even more attractive. She added quilted pillows in a rainbow of colors to the off-white couch and to the two overstuffed green chairs by the fireplace. She'd bought two small side tables for each chair and found a matching coffee table to place in front of the couch, all for sale at a furniture store Hazel wanted to show her. Best of all, she'd found a painting to go over the fireplace mantel. One that reminded her of David's family park, featuring flowers and a stone bench.

She placed the flowers David had given her on the coffee table and stood back to admire them. They were ideal. As she stared at them, she wondered if Petals, the local flower shop, needed help on the weekends. If she was going to make a change from depending on her sister, that might be a better way to earn extra money than working at the café. She'd have to see how the school year went before adding more work to her schedule.

After adding the finishing touches to the room, Misty loaded the box of trash into her car and went to the dump. In a small town like theirs, the local dump was often a source for exchanging trash for usable items people placed to one side for anyone who wanted them.

When she arrived, she parked by the entrance, carried her box over to the trash section, and studied the pile of old furniture and items off to the side. She picked up a small metal and glass table for the deck. A fresh coat of paint would make it seem like new.

Carrying her treasure to her car, Misty was thrilled by how the day was turning out.

When Misty entered Jake's that evening and saw all her friends, any idea of going to bed early fled. This group filled her world with their friendliness and kindness.

Ross Roberts spoke as she sat at one of the large tables. "Looks like we're going to have another softball game fundraiser. I'll be acting as an umpire, nothing more. But I can't vouch for what my fiancée will do."

Several people laughed. Melissa had run into Ross at the last baseball fundraiser, causing an injury that required him to have knee replacement surgery.

"You'll have to choose your teammates wisely," commented Melissa, causing more laughter.

David didn't appear, but Misty was happy to talk and joke around with other friends. She especially liked how Nettie and Jason fit into the group. Nettie had even volunteered to play ball. It was important because owning the Café meant participating actively in the local activities.

Taylor announced that following the game, a summer picnic for the players would be held at the Lilac Lake Cottage that her grandmother, GG, had given her and her two sisters.

"Everybody bring a dish to share; we'll supply the rest," said Taylor.

Dirk's fiancée, Samantha Waters, offered to handle publicity for the game. She was a marketing person who'd given up her job in Washington, D.C., to move in with Dirk. And though she was still getting used to small-town living, she was easy to be with.

Misty prepared to leave the group right after Hazel left with Mike Dawson. As Ross's partner in the sports center and a former tennis star, Mike was a little intense but seemed to get along well with Hazel. Misty was happy to see it.

As she headed out, Whitney said, "Why don't Nick and I give you a ride home?"

"Thanks," said Misty, aware of their protection, reminding her of the marked-up books and how threatened she still felt by Vince. Determined to focus on something else, Misty eagerly told Whitney about her find at the dump. She couldn't let unhappy memories destroy the new life she was creating for herself.

A few days later, as she'd done each morning, Misty got up,

walked to "David's Park" for a few moments of reflection, and then walked into town for coffee. Too soon, school would start, and she'd lose the opportunity to do so.

This morning, the sun was rising in a pinkish dawn, part of an expected heat wave underway. She dressed in shorts and a tank top, put on her walking shoes and socks, grabbed a sports towel and her phone, and headed out.

The humid air clung to her like a soggy wool sweater, but she kept moving. If she were lucky, David would be at the park. She wanted to make sure he was all right because he hadn't been to Jake's in a while.

When she reached the entrance, she saw David talking to the red-haired woman as they studied one of the flower beds. He looked up, saw her, and waved.

She went over to him. "Hi, nice to see you here. We've missed you at Jake's."

"Yes, sorry, I've been busy doing some landscaping work at The Meadows," he said, smiling at her. "Meet my mother, Susie Graham. Mom, this is Misty Owens."

His mother held out her hand, and Misty shook it. "It's nice to meet you."

Susie said, "You're Crystal Owens' younger sister. Right?"

"Yes, I am," said Misty.

"I've been staying close to home these past few years," said David's mother. "It seems a lot of young people are returning to town. It's nice to meet you. You were here in the park a few days ago, weren't you?"

"Yes. It's a beautiful spot in our town. I was sorry to hear of your daughter's death. This garden is such a lovely tribute."

"I think so, too." His mother's eyes filled as she patted David on the back. "We have David to thank for it. He put together the plan and carried it out. He and Lily were very close."

"I told Misty a little about it," said David quietly, giving me a steady look.

His mother looked from her son to Misty. "Well, you can imagine how I feel not to have my daughter around. Come visit anytime."

Surprised but pleased, Misty said, "Thank you. That's very nice."

"Years ago, I knew your mother," said Susie. "It's a long story from my nursing days. Someday, I'd like to talk to you about it."

"I'd like that," said Misty, even more surprised.

David's mother left, and Misty sat on one of the benches.

"Let me finish up here, and then I'll drive you into town," said David. "We can grab a cup of coffee together."

"Thanks. That'll be great. It's too hot to work or walk for any distance."

"Agreed," he said, smiling at her.

As she waited for him, her thoughts flew to her mother. She couldn't imagine what David's mother had to say about her.

"Ready? Let's go," said David, waving her forward.

She went to his truck and climbed in. Even though it was

only a few blocks to the Café, Misty was grateful for the ride. She'd already planned to order iced coffee.

She studied the sky. Only a thunderstorm would clear the humidity, but though there were clouds on the horizon, they didn't look threatening. Maybe this would be a pleasant lake day.

She mentioned it to David, and he grinned. "Let's call Taylor and see if we can come for a swim."

"She's told all of us that we're welcome to come use the waterfront anytime. Today's perfect."

David parked his truck, and they walked inside the Café. At the sight of Taylor working at the table in the corner, David grinned. "You ask Taylor. I'll get us coffee."

Misty asked him to get her an iced decaf mocha and headed to the back of the café.

Taylor looked up and smiled pleasantly. "Morning. You're here early."

"David and I are grabbing coffee. We were wondering if we could go swimming at your cottage. We won't be in your way. We just want to cool off, and the rock by your place is great for drying off after a swim."

"Of course," said Taylor. "Maybe I'll join you. Cooper is home, and we can all play hooky. It's that kind of day. If you see anyone else, invite them."

"Okay. I'll go home and get some things. I'll bring water and plenty of snacks."

"Great. This is going to be fun. I'm having trouble writing, and this break is just what I need."

David walked over to them and handed Misty her glass of iced coffee. "Is it a go?"

Taylor gave him a thumbs up. "A perfect summer day. I'm going home to tell Cooper. See you soon."

As Taylor started to pack up, Misty walked out of the Café with David.

After patiently waiting for Misty to change into her bikini and fill a small cooler with bottles of water, sodas, and snacks, David drove them to the cottage Taylor owned with her two sisters.

Taylor greeted them. "Cooper and I have decided to make this an impromptu summer party this afternoon. Thank you for coming, and thanks for the goodies. Whitney is making a couple of salads, and Dani is bringing hot dogs and rolls. Heaven knows what everyone else is bringing, but I'm not worried. It always works out."

Cooper appeared. Tall with chocolate-brown hair and hazel eyes behind the horn-rimmed glasses he wore, he'd become a favorite at Jake's, where his wry humor made them laugh. David, too, had a fun sense of humor. But then, it was a group that worked hard and played hard.

Cooper and David shook hands. "A day off? Cooper asked him.

"Yes. At this time of summer, when it's this hot, we try to

give our staff weekends off when we can," said David. "Fall is a busy time for us."

"I've got coffee, water, juice, and sodas set up in the kitchen," said Taylor. "Help yourself. Cooper is going to get some beer for later."

Outside, Misty stood a moment, gazing at the three-story, gray-shingled house. For years it had been known as a spooky house with a real ghost. After Taylor's grandmother gave her and her sisters the house with the promise to fix it up and live in it for at least six months every year, they'd changed it completely, including getting rid of the ghost.

Now, it was a gorgeous home with a light, contemporary feel inside. Collister Construction had done the renovation work, and Whitney and Taylor had coordinated the décor. With Dani living with Brad at the Meadows and Whitney sharing Nick's house in town, Taylor was given the task of living in the cottage for the designated time. When she and Cooper were in New York City, where they lived, Whitney and Dani often used the cottage as a retreat.

Misty helped herself to a bottle of cold water and held it to her forehead. "It's hot. I'm ready for a swim."

"Go ahead. I'll join you shortly," said Taylor. "David, why don't you grab something to drink and go on down to the rock with Misty? I'll get things organized here."

David gave her a little salute. "Are you sure I can't help with something?"

Taylor shook her head. "There's little to do at the moment.

Later, you can help Cooper with the grilling. It's going to be an easy picnic."

Misty held up the beach bag she'd brought. "I've got an extra towel for you, David."

"Thanks. I'm wearing my swim trunks beneath my shorts. So, I'm all set." He took hold of the beach bag, grabbed a bottle of water, and left the house with Misty.

The green lawn rolled down to the edge of the lake, where a huge granite rock sat half in the water. For as long as she could remember, the kids in town had used it for sunning after a swim in the lake. It had been far enough away from the ghost-inhabited cottage to feel safe during the years the cottage was neglected.

As they got closer, Misty noticed some ducks paddling among the reeds at the end of the lake. They moved listlessly as if they, too, were weighed down by the heat and humidity.

Misty climbed onto the rock and sat, keeping her cover-up on. She dreaded the moment she'd have to remove it before getting into the water. Vince had picked apart her figure, finding her flaws and using them to make her feel she was ugly. In her heart, she knew that wasn't true, but he'd been so cruel and convincing, and she'd never felt the same about her body.

"C'mon, let's go in," said David. He stood and took off his shorts, exposing a pair of red swim trunks.

Misty studied his trim, muscular body and was relieved it didn't have the shape of someone who worked out daily to bulk up. Vince had done that and sometimes flexed his muscles to intimidate her.

David held out his hand to her.

Misty caught her lip and slipped out of the cover-up, holding her breath. When she glanced at him, she noticed his look of admiration and told herself to relax.

David stopped and faced her with a look of concern. "You're trembling. What's wrong?"

Misty closed her eyes to hold in the sting of tears. "Nothing. Old memories."

"Look at me," said David softly.

Misty opened her eyes and found herself drawn into David's blue-eyed gaze. "Whatever it is, I want you to know I'm here for you."

"Thanks. I'm not ready to talk about it. But, someday, I hope I will be."

They walked down to the water's edge and dove in, bodies outstretched as they headed for depth.

"Ah, that feels good," said David, re-emerging and shaking a lock of blond-streaked hair out of his face. He dove beneath the surface and swam away from her.

She swam after him and laughed when he sprang up at her and caught her in his arms before quickly letting her go.

"Race you back," he said and took off.

Misty followed, and they reached the rock at the same time.

He offered her a hand, and she took it, allowing him to pull her up to the flat surface.

She handed him a towel and quickly dried off so she could put on her cover-up. She'd just lifted it when David said, "Don't you want to enjoy the sun?"

Not knowing what to say, she shrugged.

He frowned. "I hope this has nothing to do with how you look. My sister always worried about that, and, like her, you're beautiful."

Misty's cheeks felt hot as she let the cover-up fall. Silently, she laid her beach towel out on the rock's surface and sat down. Staring out at the water, she remained quiet.

David put a hand on her shoulder. "Anytime you want to talk about it, I'm here. I'm a good listener."

She turned to him. "Thanks. I thought I was doing okay until something happened recently."

Taylor's arrival ended their conversation, but Misty felt as if David's comforting words had wrapped around her like a protective embrace.

Throughout the morning, more and more people arrived. Only Dirk with his dental patients, Emmett with his medical practice, and Nick as sheriff were tied to their jobs. Most everyone else had enough time to stop by for lunch or to stay awhile.

Misty appreciated that Mike had picked up Hazel and brought her for lunch.

After lunch, David offered her a ride home, and Misty took

it. As nice as it was to swim and sun, she'd had enough.

David was quiet as he drove to her cabin. But after he pulled into the driveway, he said quietly, "Do you feel safe here?"

Misty studied the cabin. "Yes. Thank you for asking."

He waited for her to say something more, but she couldn't mention Vince's name. It would bring back all her past bad memories, and once she started telling him about them, she wouldn't be able to stop. And she didn't want to seem weak in David's eyes.

CHAPTER FOUR

THE NEXT MORNING, AFTER A FEROCIOUS THUNDERSTORM during the night, Misty decided to forego her walk to the park. She was troubled by her conversations with David. He was aware something bad had happened in her past, but she wasn't ready to share details with him. When she'd returned to Lilac Lake, she'd still been in a state of shock while she'd talked to Crystal and Emmett about it. She'd seen a counselor and had thought she was learning how to deal with everything Vince had put her through. Now, she knew she still had some underlying issues to resolve. It would take work, but she had to do it no matter how painful it was.

A few days later, David called. "I'm wondering if you'd like to come to dinner at my parent's house on Sunday. My mother specifically asked me to invite you."

Misty was intrigued by the short conversation she'd had with his mother. "Thanks. I'd like that. What time do you want me there?"

"I'll pick you up at five. All right?"

"Yes. That's fine. I'll be ready."

"I've been wanting to call you, but one of our guys quit, and I've been busy doing the landscaping myself for a house at The Meadows. Will I see you at Jake's tonight?"

"Yes. It's a great way to relax at the end of the day. And I love their salads. An easy dinner."

"Great. See you there. Remember, we have the softball game on Saturday. You're on my team."

"I know. I'm warning you that you may be sorry, but I'll try my best." Misty hadn't played much softball.

"It'll be fun," said David. "This time, we're playing the girls softball team from Dartmouth. We'll need all the help we can get. Mike will be there, of course, and Ben is coming up from Washington D.C.. But we could only get a couple of girls from the high school team to help us." Ben Gooding was another former professional baseball player and a friend of Ross's.

"It'll all be worth it if it raises money for the sports center," Misty said.

"I think so, too," said David. "I have to go, but I'll see you tonight."

Misty ended the call and stared at the lesson plans she was working on for her second-grade class. She was anxious to have things in order because she knew the chaos of running a classroom. It is best to be prepared.

Thinking of the school year ahead, Misty wondered how students here might differ from the older students she had taught in Florida. But then, kids were the same everywhere. She was delighted that her students would be from a variety of backgrounds and hard-working families.

That night, when she and Hazel were at Jake's, David approached the table, keeping his eyes on Misty, and she felt a flush of pleasure.

Ben made room for him at the table, and David greeted everyone. "You talking about the game? I heard that one of the Dartmouth baseball stars can't make it."

"Yeah, I heard that, too," said Ben. "But they have plenty of other excellent players. We'll still struggle, but we'll be all right."

"Yeah, we've got a lot of determination on our side," said Ross. "That'll count for something." He put his arm around Melissa. "And don't forget we have an excellent player right here."

Melissa laughed. "We'll see. I'm going to try my best not to run into anyone."

"It'll be great to play on the new baseball field," said David.

"I've arranged for a couple of food trucks to come to the game," said Crystal. "That should add to the fun."

Gray clouds filled the sky on Saturday morning when Misty awoke. Worried, she went to her window and peered out. She couldn't see any signs of a storm, just gray skies. Hopefully, it would stay that way, even though an afternoon storm was predicted. Cooler nights had reminded her of early signs of upcoming fall weather with the recent heat wave over. Now, they could play their benefit game in comfort.

For their last fundraiser, Ross had coached members of his team ahead of game time. Even though he'd offered to do it again, nobody, including Misty, had taken him up on it. Feeling her nerves kick in, she wished she had.

The rest of the team was there when she arrived. She waved, parked her car, and walked over to them. Melissa came over and handed her a baseball glove. "Great to see you. The Dartmouth team is here, and they look like real pros."

The women from Dartmouth wore white uniforms with green trim, dark green knee socks, and green visors. Seeing how professional they looked, Misty felt intimidated.

Melissa put a hand on her shoulder. "Don't worry. We have a few surprise moves planned."

The game began with the toss of a coin. Dartmouth won and opted to bat first. Misty suspected they just wanted to test how bad their opponents were. With Ben playing first base and Melissa in center field, they'd have a stronger defense than she'd thought. She was pleasantly surprised when Mike took the position of pitcher.

After a few tense moments, the first half of the first inning ended with Dartmouth scoring just one run.

Dirk was up first when it was time for her team to bat. He hit a ground ball and was called out at first. Next, Melissa hit a fly ball that was easily caught, and Misty, feeling the pressure, struck out.

They were in the fifth inning of the game when the storm clouds hovering in the sky broke loose with thunder and lightning. With a score of four to one, Dartmouth was declared the winner as everyone scattered after Taylor announced she'd move the picnic to another day.

Crystal huddled in Misty's car as raindrops smacked the windshield with angry slaps. "Luckily, the food trucks did a fantastic lunch business before the storm," she said. "I'm testing their use for Ross and Mike's sports center."

"It was a fun game," said Misty. "And having food here was a great idea. I feel that the sports center is going to be a huge success. It'll be very versatile."

Misty dropped Crystal off at her house and went home to change out of her damp clothes. The thought of curling up on the couch with a book was enticing. Tomorrow, she'd have dinner with David and his family. She was already nervous.

As part of her Sunday routine, Misty did laundry and prepared a list of groceries for meals for the following week. She'd learned it helped to have things organized both at home and at school when she was teaching.

But her thoughts never strayed too far from the upcoming dinner with David and his family. She wondered if his mother would tell her about knowing the woman who'd given Misty birth. Her memories of her mother weren't pleasant, though she could recall a few occasions when she'd paid attention to her. But even then, she'd known something was wrong with her mother's behavior.

Misty was more than ready when David came to pick her up. She'd dressed in a pretty sundress and had shampooed her dark hair, leaving it shiny and straight. Her facial features were a blend of Crystal's and those of a man she didn't know and never had. Another reason Misty was anxious to hear David's mother's story.

"Wow! You look beautiful!" said David, seeing her. His look of delight lit his blue eyes, drawing her attention. A flush of heat warmed her cheeks. After her experience with Vince, she was always surprised when someone mentioned her appearance positively.

"Ready?" David asked her.

"Yes. Just let me grab my purse," she replied, taking hold of it and heading to the door. Outside, she paused and carefully locked the front door.

David held the car door for her before going around the truck and sliding behind the wheel. "My parents' house is across the lake from the Inn. It's a little quieter on our side of the lake."

"You told me you lived at home to be with your sister. Do you still live there?"

"No, I have a small place on the land we own behind the cottage. We have acreage on the opposite side of the lake road that we use for a nursery to grow a lot of our plants. We originally built a place for a manager to oversee it, but I've taken over the job and the space."

"Graham Landscaping is a much bigger operation than one would think," said Misty.

"Yes, it's grown a lot. Aaron Collister owns acreage in that area, too. He has a maple grove that he uses for his maple sugar production. It's a cool setup."

"He lives there too?" she asked.

"Temporarily. He's building a house in a far corner of The Meadows development," said David. "I may eventually move there too. I've bought a lot, in case I want to do that. Aaron and I share a love of nature and have been friends for years. He gave me a deal on the land."

"It's nice to have that flexibility," Misty said.

"My parents want me to take over the cottage for them. They're looking to downsize," said David. "I'm not sure what I want to do. They've got a big place."

"I feel very lucky to have the cabin. It was sweet of Crystal to give me a room in her apartment when I first returned, but I love living on my own."

"Yeah, me too," said David. He headed down a long, paved driveway to a large, two-story building with a white clapboard exterior.

Misty stared at it, realizing the word "cottage" was a deceiving description. Even from the rear of the house, Misty could see the end of what she thought must be a sweeping front porch, and she studied the three greenhouse windows in what she guessed must be the kitchen.

David pulled up to the paved parking area beside a three-car garage. "Well, here we are. Come on in."

Before they could reach the house, David's mother greeted them at the door.

"Welcome! I'm very happy you could come, Misty. It's a beautiful day."

"Thank you, Mrs. Graham. I'm happy to be invited."

David's mother waved away her formality. "Please call me Susie. Come inside. David's father is watching the end of the Red Sox game. They're losing, but there's always hope."

Misty entered a back entry hall that served as a mud room and entered the up-to-date kitchen that had a homey, country feel to it. The three window greenhouses on the outside wall added a pleasant touch of greenery. An island with bar stools lined up on one side filled the center of the room, and two long interior walls held appliances and white cabinetry.

One end of the room opened into a dining area, which opened to the living room. A riverstone fireplace sat on the exterior wall between the dining and living rooms, adding a warm touch to each.

At the sound of their approach, a tall, gray-haired man rose from the leather couch and turned to face them. A smile lit his tanned, weathered face, and he walked over to them.

"Hi, you must be Misty Owens all grown up," he said. "I'm Rod. I'm glad you could join us. It's nice to have a young woman in the house again."

"Thanks for inviting me," Misty said, noting the sadness in Rod's hazel eyes.

Rod clapped a hand on David's back. "Great to have you here, son."

"Now that the game is over, let's sit in the sunroom," said Susie. "It's such a lovely day."

The four of them went to the front room, where three outside walls held large windows with views overlooking the lake. Beyond the sunroom was an open porch that curved around the corner, so the views from there were of the water or a small flower garden.

"This is very pretty," said Misty, taking a seat on the couch. "You have the best views across the lake to the Lilac Lake Inn."

"It's relaxing to see what's going on there without being part of it," said Susie. "It's nice now that the Inn has been renovated."

"How about something to drink before dinner?" Rod said. "We have beer and wine or something stronger."

"Or lemonade, if you prefer," said Susie.

"A glass of wine would be lovely," Misty said. "Red, if you have it."

"I have a nice Chandler Hill Inn pinot noir," said Rod. "Sus, does that suit you?"

"Lovely," she said, smiling at him.

Misty looked out the front windows and saw a boathouse on the shore.

"That's where we keep a canoe and a fishing boat," said David, who'd noticed her looking at it.

"It's a beautiful property," Misty said. "Everything's right here."

"It's getting a little large for us," said Susie. "We're hoping the day will come when David wants to take it over so we can move to a smaller house with less upkeep."

"I'm not ready, and I don't think you're quite ready for retirement. Are you?" said David, looking at his father.

Rod shook his head. "Not yet, but I don't want to wait until it's too late to enjoy it. But I'm slowing down, which is why I'm satisfied you're more or less in charge now."

"Some days more in charge, some days less," said David, making his father laugh.

Misty listened to the conversation, enjoying the gentle sparring between the two men. Having had no father in her life, she didn't know what to expect.

Susie caught Misty's eye and gave her a wide smile.

Misty returned it and accepted the glass of wine Rod handed her.

After everyone had been served, Rod lifted his glass. "Here's to life."

As she held up her glass, Susie blinked back tears and murmured, "To life."

Touched by how it must affect David's parents to say that after losing their daughter, Misty joined in. "To life."

Sitting next to her on the couch, David touched his glass to hers.

The conversation turned to Misty's job and eventually to matters in town, including the restaurant called Refresh by the owners of Fresh, who were taking over the space vacated by Fins.

"We might join the Hendricksons in Florida for a couple of weeks next winter," said Susie. "We'll see. After losing Fins, I believe they're planning on staying there for the entire season."

"I loved Florida, but this is a better place for me right now," said Misty. No way she was going to mention her trouble with Vince. She didn't want David's parents to know how stupid she'd been, especially when they had a son as kind and supportive as David.

"I hope you enjoy steak," said Rod. "I've got some beautiful strip steaks marinating. I'll get those grilled whenever you're ready, Susie."

"In time. I'm enjoying the company," Susie said in an easygoing manner. She turned to Misty. "Tell me about the cabin you're renting. I heard they were cute, and the location couldn't be better."

Misty described it and said how nice it was to live close to Hazel so they could travel back and forth to school together.

"And what will you wear to school? I know fashion is much more casual. Lily taught school for a couple of years before she got sick. She always loved working with the kids but said pants were more comfortable because of how active she was."

Rod stood. "While you women talk clothes, David and I will check on the grill. Okay?"

"Sure," said Susie. "Everything else is ready to serve. Let me know when the grill is ready, and we'll go from there. In the meantime, I'll enjoy some girl time."

After the men left to go outside, Susie turned to Misty. "I'm so happy we have a chance to chat. I've missed them with my daughter. It also allows me to tell you what I know about your mother. It's not much, but it's something that I think is important for you to hear."

Misty sat anxiously on the edge of her seat.

"Years ago, I worked occasionally as a maternity nurse at the Portsmouth Regional Hospital. That's how I met your mother. She was there for prenatal care and delivery." Susie gave her a tender look. "She was so excited about having you and worked hard to remain sober during the pregnancy. And she was thrilled when you were born. She thought you would help her straighten out her life."

"But when I was old enough to realize something was wrong, it was clear that her life hadn't changed," said Misty, trying to absorb Susie's words.

"All I know is that she tried. She really tried. I met with her a couple of times after you were born, but soon, she refused to talk about her life, and there was nothing I could do beyond helping her get into treatment programs, which I did a couple of times."

"Do you know who my father is?" Misty asked.

Susie shook her head. "No. Your mother wouldn't talk about him. I'm not sure she knew. But I wanted you to understand that no matter what else happened, you were loved and wanted. Every child needs to hear that."

Tears stung Misty's eyes. "Thank you. I'm glad you told me."

Susie came over to the couch and sat beside her. Gazing at her, she said, "I hope we can become friends. It would mean so much to me."

Misty studied the gentle expression on Susie's face and realized Susie needed this connection as much as she did. Wordlessly, they hugged one another.

Tears wet Susie's cheeks when they pulled apart, and Misty knew Susie was thinking of her daughter.

Clasping Susie's hand, Misty said, "Now, how about that girl talk? Ask me anything you want."

Soon, they were laughing as Misty told Susie about the plant David had given her for the cabin and how she said a little prayer of thanks each morning it lived.

"I seem to lack a green thumb," said Misty.

"Sweet words of love can do wonders," Susie said. "It's that way about life, too."

David approached them. "Dad says the grill is hot. Okay if he starts to cook the steaks?"

Misty and Susie glanced at one another and nodded. Misty thought they both might be ready for something more than one dinner together.

51

CHAPTER FIVE

As he drove her home, David was quiet. Misty was content to let the silence between them continue. She had a lot on her mind.

David pulled into the driveway, stopped the engine, and turned to her. "I haven't seen my mother this happy in a long time. She misses Lily, and your visit has done her a world of good."

"She helped me too. While we were in the kitchen, she asked me to meet her for lunch before the start of school, and I said I would. With no mother, I've never had the chance to do something like that."

"Nice," said David. His gaze settled on her and softened as he pulled her close. Tilting her chin, he met her lips with his own, sending warmth and something more through her.

Memories suddenly blocked her senses. Vince used to pin her arms and whisper ugly words into her ear.

Misty fought the feeling of being trapped in David's embrace. Heart pounding, she pushed him away. "I'm sorry. I can't."

David gave her a look of concern. "Are you alright? Is it anything I did?"

Tears blurred her vision. "It's not you. I'm not ready for more. Not yet."

"Look, we don't have to do this, but I want to continue seeing you. May I call you? Ask you out?" David asked.

"I'd like that, but only if you're willing to be patient with me." She climbed out of David's car and turned to him. She gave him a tentative smile and waved. She couldn't let Vince ruin what she felt with David. Nobody had ever kissed her like that.

He waved and smiled in return, and after waiting to see that she got inside the house okay, he pulled out of the driveway.

Misty waited until he was gone, and then she shut the front door and leaned against it. She realized how demanding and controlling Vinnie had been, even when kissing her. She'd mistaken that for passion. Now, after David's kiss, she knew better.

The next morning, Misty decided to visit the park. It seemed only right after spending the night thinking about David's family. His mother was such a loving person, and it touched Misty to think Susie genuinely wanted to spend time with her. She'd always be grateful to her for sharing the story about her mother. It was a precious gift to know her mother wanted her, even under unusual circumstances.

Misty hugged her pillow. No wonder David was such a

caring person. He'd come from a warm family who'd shown him what love was. And that kiss of his was magical. If only she hadn't allowed thoughts of her toxic ex to intrude on the moment.

She got out of bed and dressed for her morning walk. She had only a short time before she had to set up her classroom and attend orientation classes for new teachers. Students would arrive for their first day of school on August 28th. Until then, Misty planned to take advantage of every summer day she could.

She was now familiar with the neighborhood that she walked through to get to the garden and waved to an older woman who was watering her flowers in front of her house. Farther down the block, a fluffy white dog ran to the front fence of his house, barking a greeting. Most of the rest of the houses had little activity as she walked along the sidewalk early this morning.

In the garden, Misty was relieved to see that no one was there. She wanted the place for herself to reflect upon the family who'd created this space for the town. Misty wanted to show her respect to the young woman after being with the Grahams, seeing photographs of his sister, and knowing of their love for Lily.

She lowered herself onto one of the park benches and stared at the pink flowers in front of her. She was certain she would've liked Lily. Misty hadn't known her except as a pretty young woman who was older than Crystal's group of friends.

She'd left town for college in New York City, and, following graduation, had stayed in New York doing some modeling before becoming a teacher. With her blond beauty, Lily might never have chosen Misty as a friend, and yet Misty felt connected to her in a way she couldn't describe.

A butterfly landed on a pink rose and then fluttered its wings in front of Misty's face for a few seconds before flying away. She could almost believe it was a sign from Lily to follow her instincts and reach out to Lily's mother.

Thinking of Susie, Misty wondered if David's mother was how all mothers were supposed to be. Crystal had done more than most sisters would to keep the two of them together as a family the state couldn't tear apart. However, although she was a wonderful sister to Misty, Crystal was not her mother.

Misty bowed her head and silently promised Lily she'd do what she could to bring Susie some happiness. An image of David came to her mind. He was the reason she dared to stretch herself emotionally. He was showing her how a decent man acts, allowing her to believe in her self-worth.

She heard someone moving toward her and lifted her head to see David.

He waved and sat beside her. "I hoped I'd find you here. Thanks again for coming for dinner." He gave her a shy smile. "And for ... everything. I'm sincere about wanting to see you again. I'll be patient, I promise."

"I loved being with you and your family," Misty said. "It's difficult when painful memories take over. I don't often talk about what went on with my ex-boyfriend, but it's all there in my head. I'm working on getting past it."

"I'll be there for you every step of the way," he said. "I believe we can have something special between us. I felt it when you came back to town but knew you needed time to adjust."

"Thanks for understanding," she said. "I truly want to spend more time with you."

"That's something we agree on." He stood. "I've got to go to work, but like I said, I'll call you, and we can have a real date."

"That sounds like fun," she said, feeling almost giddy about his understanding. Vince would never have been so kind, so patient.

She stayed a little longer in the park before heading into town for her usual coffee at the Café. When she arrived there, Nettie and Crystal greeted her together. She knew Crystal was helping Nettie establish a typical café routine in preparation for Labor Day Weekend, which was fast approaching.

"How did your dinner go with the Grahams?" Crystal asked her.

"It went well. When we have some time alone, I'll tell you about it. Susie Graham knew our mother briefly."

Crystal frowned. "I know Mrs. Graham helped Mom once or twice when you were small, but usually, Mom refused any help. Especially as her addiction took control of her life."

"I'll share the entire conversation with you later," said

Misty.

Instead of going on her way as usual, Misty sat on a stool at the counter, soaking up the conversations around her, enjoying being part of a small-town morning at the café. Where would she be today if she hadn't grown up here? She'd needed to leave town for a while before she could truly appreciate Lilac Lake and the people who lived here.

Nettie joined her. "Remember, you're welcome to work here on a part-time basis on the weekends, most especially for any gourmet dinners."

"Thanks, I appreciate that. I want to immerse myself in my school activities, so I won't be available for a while except for the gourmet dinners. Those will be too much fun to miss."

"Great," said Nettie, clapping her on the shoulder. "When your sister said the café was successfully busy, I had no idea how true it would be. I'm in love with this town and these people. I thought I might have to work at the Inn, but I don't see how I can. I'm too busy here."

"What about Jason? Is he working here full-time?" Misty asked.

"He's cooking at Fresh on the weekends and will work at the new restaurant, Refresh, when they get it up and running."

"You're both becoming a real part of the town. That's very important." Misty picked up her coffee to go and decided to check out her classroom in the school to see what else she might need.

That afternoon, she looked at the list of learning games and workbooks she'd bought online. Second grade, like all the primary grades, was important as a time to encourage the joy of learning. She loved it when the kids got excited about learning a new skill, a new thought.

At the sound of the doorbell, Misty hurried to open it. She and Hazel had talked, and Hazel wanted to see what she'd bought.

When she opened the door, she was surprised to see a man holding onto a glass vase of yellow roses, a symbol, she knew, of friendship.

"Hello," the man said. "Mrs. Graham sent me. These flowers are for you."

"Oh, thank you." Misty accepted the vase from him, touched by the sweet gesture. She knew how much their talk yesterday had meant to Susie. It had meant a lot to her, too.

She opened the note and read: *Thank you for your kind understanding. I'm looking forward to having lunch with you.*

As the man got into his truck, Hazel approached. "Wow! What gentleman is sending you flowers?"

Misty shook her head. "They're from David's mother, not him. It's a thank-you of sorts. She's been very lonely, missing her daughter. And I love talking with her. It's almost like I imagine it would be if I had a mother."

"How sweet!" Hazel said and followed Misty inside.

Misty led Hazel to the kitchen, where she'd placed a list of items she'd bought: books, puzzles, dot-to-dot coloring books, crayons, pencils, erasers, and a few special items.

"I have so much to show you. A lot of the stores are offering teacher discounts, and I took advantage of them."

Hazel studied the list of items Misty had selected. "Looks like you're as excited as I am to start the school year. These are all wonderful additions to your other teaching resources."

"I'll fill in with them where necessary," said Misty. "I don't want any child to feel left out." She remembered all too well how awful she'd felt when she didn't have the supplies other kids brought to school and how her teachers had made sure she did.

After they'd sorted through everything, Misty said, "Want to plan a shopping trip for clothes? We can go to the outlet malls in Maine. Or anywhere else you want." She knew money wasn't an issue for Hazel.

"Sure, let's go tomorrow. I need practical things to wear in the classroom."

"That'll be fun," said Misty. "What are you up to this evening? Going to Jake's?"

"Mike has asked me out to dinner at Stan's. I said I'd go if we didn't make it a late evening. I want to be well rested before I go home for a visit next week."

"A last trip south for a while," said Misty. "Do you miss New Orleans?"

"We live outside the city, but I miss the food there. I love

Lilac Lake, though. It's where I want to settle."

"I understand," said Misty. "Lilac Lake is a special place. And I think a certain gentleman is smitten with you."

"You mean Mike?" Hazel asked. "He's a great guy, but we're not seriously dating. I'm not ready for that."

"New people are moving into town all the time," said Misty, realizing she wasn't interested in dating anyone but David. With him, she felt safe. And she loved his family.

Misty was finishing hanging up her new clothes when her cell rang. *David.*

"Hi," she said, her heart beating a happy tattoo.

"Hi. I said I'd call. I wonder if you want to come to my house tomorrow for dinner. We can watch a movie afterward if you want to. Are you into Super Heroes?"

Misty grinned. "I think they're fun."

"Great. I'll be working late, but I can pick you up at seven."

"That will be perfect," Misty said, eager to be upbeat and not let bad memories get in the way of a relationship with this incredible man.

"Did you have a nice day?" he asked politely.

Misty told him about her shopping trip with Hazel. "Now that it's getting close to school time, I'm getting excited."

"The kids you teach are going to be very lucky," he said. "I still remember my second-grade teacher, Mrs. Gilbert. She was very kind about helping me with math. I didn't realize how much I'd need it for my work."

"That's such a nice story. I hope to be a teacher just like that."

"I have a feeling you will be," said David. "I've got to go, but I'll see you tomorrow. Thanks."

Misty ended the call smiling. David's support meant everything to her.

CHAPTER SIX

THE NEXT DAY, THE RAINY MORNING KEPT MISTY FROM her usual routine of walking to the park and into town for coffee. She decided to make a lazy morning of it and stayed in her pajamas, working on posters to hang in her classroom. Her theme for the year was going to be kindness. Like everyone else, second-grade students needed a safe space, and she wanted her students to be sure that everyone would be treated well in her classroom.

Hazel showed up.

Misty fixed her a cup of coffee and sat to chat at the kitchen table.

"I wanted to stop by before I take off for home. I'm taking an Uber to Boston's Logan Airport for my flight to New Orleans. I'll be gone for only a few days. I'm prepared for my class and will be able to attend the training sessions for teachers as scheduled."

"It'll be nice to see family, I'm sure," said Misty. "And don't worry about a thing here. I'll keep an eye on your cabin."

"Thanks. I appreciate it."

Misty walked Hazel to the front door, grateful for her friendship.

For the rest of the day, Misty kept busy with projects while the thoughts of going to David's house for dinner filled her mind. She felt comfortable with him, yet the idea of being alone at his house kept her on edge. She hadn't dated anyone since returning to Lilac Lake, and the thought of being with him both excited and worried her.

When David came to pick her up, his hair damp from a shower, her jitters evaporated. He'd taken care to put on clean clothes, and a smell of lemony citrus aftershave wafted gently around him.

"Right on time," she said and grabbed her purse.

"You look great," he said.

Her cheeks flushed, flattered by his compliment. She'd chosen to wear a long, flowing turquoise skirt with a white V-neck top that showed off the silver and turquoise necklace she wore.

He walked her to the driveway. He used a white truck with the Graham Landscaping banner on it during the day, but on his own, he drove a smaller, silver truck.

David helped her inside, went around the back of the truck, and got behind the wheel.

They saw JoEllen emerge from her cabin. When she saw them, she signaled for them to stop.

David pulled his truck up to her.

"Are you going to Jake's?" JoEllen asked him.

"No," said David. "But if you're going there, have fun."

JoEllen glanced from him to Misty and back.

Before she could ask any questions, David gave JoEllen a quick wave and took off.

"I suppose everyone will know we were seen together," said Misty.

"Does that bother you?" asked David, studying her.

She shook her head. "No."

"I'm glad. That's how it should be. Sooner or later, everyone will know more details, but for the time being, let's enjoy the evening."

Misty realized David was only eight years older than she, but he seemed much older. Maybe because he was at peace with himself.

As he drove, David said, "Dinner won't be fancy. As you learned the other day at my parent's house, I know how to grill."

"Whatever it is, I'm sure it'll be delicious. The best thing is I don't have to cook."

He frowned. "But I thought you were a great cook. You helped at the café."

"Yes, I can cook things in quantity and with easy orders, but preparing dinner for myself day after day is a real chore. Thank God for Jake's."

He laughed. "Amen."

Curious to see his house, Misty leaned forward as they approached the small cottage on what was clearly a landscaper's farm. Row after row of trees and bushes filled the land around the cottage. A large red barn nearby housed equipment, as seen through its half-open doorway, where the white truck was parked.

She got out and studied the landscape. "Are those Christmas trees?" she asked, pointing to a large section of spruce trees.

"Yes," said David. "Our Christmas trees are the best in the area. People come from all around to pick one. It provides a nice income for us during the slow winter months."

"It's smart to provide your own plants for landscaping work," said Misty.

"Individuals can order specific trees and bushes from us, even if we don't plant them," said David. "After graduating from Cornell, I was able to put to use a lot of new ideas for increasing productivity and income."

"I didn't realize this was such a big operation. No wonder you're busy all the time."

He grinned. "But not too busy to have fun."

She laughed. "Guess we're both ready for some fun."

She stared at the cottage. It looked a lot like her cabin, with gray clapboards and white trim. "It's cute."

"And practical. We don't want people on the land without permission. By living here, I can keep watch. And it gives me the freedom I need from living with my parents. As long as Lily was alive, I spent a lot of time at home with her. Now, with both of us out of the house, my mother has been especially lonely. I'm grateful that you and she are forming a friendship.

It's been a huge help to her."

He took hold of Misty's hand to lead her inside the cabin.

At his firm grip, she stiffened.

"Anything wrong?" he asked, giving her a look of concern.

"It's something I have to get over," she said, telling herself to relax. "Let's enjoy the evening."

They walked to the cabin, where the front porch overlooked the lake.

David led her up the steps and opened the front door.

When Misty walked inside, she immediately felt at home. The layout was similar to her cabin, with a large living and dining space and a kitchen visible from the doorway.

David showed her the master bedroom suite, the laundry/mud room, and the one-car garage, which was currently filled with equipment.

"Nothing fancy, but it's workable," said David. At the sound of whining at the back door, he went to answer it. "Meet Homer. My neighbor's dog."

He opened the door, and a big black lab stood wagging his tail at them.

"My elderly neighbor owns him. But when I'm around the cottage, Homer comes to visit me."

"He's a lot like Dani's dog," said Misty, rubbing Homer's ears.

"I've promised my neighbor that if anything happens to him, I'll take care of Homer. But, needless to say, I don't want that to happen. Besides, Lily's Dachshund, who she'd had for many years, died soon after Lily did, and neither my parents nor I are ready to take on a new dog just yet."

"I love dogs," said Misty, "but I understand you need time before getting another one."

Homer came inside and plopped himself down on the kitchen floor. David chuckled. "That's right, Homer. Just lie there in the way of everyone else."

The dog wagged his tail, thumping it against the floor happily.

"We can sit on the porch while I grill the chicken," said David. "What'll you have to drink? How does a glass of wine sound?"

"Delicious," she said, forcing herself to relax.

"I've got a nice chardonnay from Chandler Hill," said David.

"Is there anything I can do for you?" Misty asked.

"Yes. When it's time, you can toss a salad I picked up in a package. One of the pre-mixed ones from the store." He got out a bottle of wine and two glasses, then poured some wine into each glass.

She and Homer followed him out to the porch. With a sigh, Homer flopped down on the floor beside her chair.

David clinked his wine glass against hers. "I'm glad you could come tonight. With my work schedule, I'm a stay-at-home kind of guy. Right now, I want to sit with you and watch the sunset."

They were quiet as they sipped their wine and observed the

sky change colors before darkening. The fact that they were content to sit like this meant a lot to Misty. Having grown up amidst chaos, peaceful moments like these were precious to her.

David turned on the porch lights and lit the gas grill.

Misty followed him into the kitchen and watched as he seasoned the chicken pieces and then carried them out to the grill.

"When the chicken is done cooking, you can put together that salad, if you will," he said.

Happy to do something for him, she said, "No problem."

Later, Misty let out a sigh of contentment as she finished her meal. David had surprised her with a homemade barbeque sauce that he'd spread on the cooking chicken, giving it a delicious taste. And the romaine salad was a tasty addition to the simple meal.

"I've got ice cream for dessert," David said.

Misty shook her head. "Maybe later. Right now, I'm full."

"Okay, then. Movie time."

Misty followed him into the living room, where a large leather couch faced a brick fireplace and a television mounted on the wall above the mantel. She sat on the couch and waited while he signed in for a movie, and then they both leaned back against the cushion to watch.

The fast-moving story and action of the superheroes were

amusing.

When David moved closer to her, she didn't mind. But when he put an arm around her and pulled her closer, she fought the urge to push him away.

He sensed something was wrong and turned to her with a frown. "What's wrong?"

Misty shivered. "I'm just sensitive about feeling trapped by anyone."

"Good God! Is that how you think of me? As someone trapping you?" His look of hurt stung her.

He moved his arm away.

"No, no. Wait. Believe me, it's not you. But with what's gone on in the past, I'm still trying to get over that feeling."

He stared at her with understanding. "I promise never to hurt you."

Her eyes filled. "I know that, but that old fear sometimes surprises me."

"Whatever it takes, I'll help you through it," said David. His voice was full of kindness, and Misty knew why he was so successful growing things and making plants and flowers thrive under his care.

She leaned her head against his shoulder, enjoying the feel of his broad shoulder beneath her, shoring her up.

He looked down at her with a tender expression. "You'll be safe with me."

Again, she fought tears but was determined not to show it. She'd been raised to be strong, to survive in a way her mother hadn't been able to.

They continued to watch the movie.

Aware of how close she was to David and how strong he was, Misty could hardly tune into the onscreen adventures. She'd thought she'd handled surviving Vince's abuse well. Now, she knew it would take more time, but David gave her hope she'd overcome the demons of her past.

After the movie ended, David said, "Are you ready for that ice cream?"

Surprised at herself, Misty said, "I think I am."

He got out chocolate-marshmallow-crunch ice cream and scooped some into two bowls.

Sitting at the table with him, enjoying the treat, Misty studied him. Handsome and kind, he was everything she'd hoped to find in a man one day. But would he have the patience to wait for her to heal from her past?

Later, David let Homer out of the cottage and walked Misty to his truck.

His hand brushed hers with every stride he took, but he didn't grab hold of it.

When Misty could stand it no more, she took hold of his hand and squeezed it, and he squeezed back.

He faced her. "I'll wait for you to let me know when you're comfortable."

"Thanks. It may seem silly, but control is very important to me. I'd lost it all."

"I think I understand," said David. "I don't know the person who did this to you, but I hope I never meet him. It would get ugly."

Misty's stomach twisted. *A meeting between David and Vince?* That would be a nightmare too horrible to contemplate.

They climbed into his truck and were silent as David drove to her cabin..

"The stars are beautiful," she finally murmured.

"Yes. It's been a nice evening," commented David, pulling up to her cabin. He turned to her with a questioning look.

"I had a great time," Misty said, unhooking her seatbelt. Then, before she could think too much about it, she leaned forward and kissed him on the lips before hopping out of the truck.

When she looked back, David was smiling as he waved goodbye.

CHAPTER SEVEN

A COUPLE OF DAYS LATER, MISTY WAITED FOR SUSIE TO pick her up for lunch. Though she'd made her comfortable at dinner at her house, they still didn't know each other that well. But Misty understood how important this was for Susie, and was excited to get to know her better. She'd even imagined this is what it might be like for other young women—lunch with her mother.

Susie pulled up to the cabin in a blue SUV, and Misty went outside to greet her.

"Hello," said Susie. "This is such a pretty area with these cabins lining the water. And you look very nice."

"Thank you," said Misty. The denim skirt and ruffled pink blouse were the fourth outfit she'd tried on.

She climbed into the car and buckled up.

"I thought we'd go to Chica's for lunch. Mama Montoya is an old friend, and their food is delicious."

"Mexican food sounds delicious," said Misty, relieved she didn't have to choose.

"You must be excited about school starting soon," said Susie. "It's always a bittersweet time, with summer ending."

"I feel lucky to have the job. There will be some teacher

training sessions, and then we begin. Soon after, we have the Labor Day holiday before we start again. That allows all of us to adjust to the new situation."

"I remember those days," said Susie, driving with confidence.

She swung into Chica's parking lot. Colorful plastic lanterns lined the perimeter of the lot, giving a sense of what the interior of the restaurant might be like.

Misty got out of the car and waited for Susie to join her.

"I haven't been here in a long time," said Misty. "But it smells the same. Delicious."

Susie smiled. "The food is always incredible. And I like to give them my business."

When they stepped inside, Mama Montoya, the owner, rushed up to them. "Susie, it's wonderful to see you, my friend. How are you? I've been holding you in my prayers since sweet Lily passed."

Misty watched the two women embrace. Mama Montoya had dark hair with streaks of gray. But her face was unlined, and her dark eyes revealed her emotions. Dressed in a colorful red skirt and a white blouse with flowers embroidered across the front, she looked the part of a hostess.

"When you called for a reservation, I put together a special little luncheon for you. Do you trust me?" Mama asked Susie.

"Do I trust you? When haven't I?" said Susie with an easy smile.

Misty followed Mama and Susie to a booth and slid onto

the red vinyl-covered bench seat facing Susie.

Mama studied her. "Such a lovely young woman. You remind me of my granddaughter, Pilar. So young and beautiful." She placed a hand on Susie's shoulder. "You be sure to ask how Susie helps our Mexican community."

"Now, Mama, that's not necessary," said Susie.

"Oh, but it is," said Mama, waving away Susie's concern. "What can I get you to drink? How about a special margarita?"

Susie gave Misty a questioning look.

"That would be nice," Misty said.

Susie said, "Make that two. This is a celebration of sorts. Me getting out in public again."

The two older women smiled at one another.

"*Bueno*," said Mama and left them.

Misty took a moment to look around the restaurant. As the outdoor lanterns had indicated, the colorful interior had bright turquoise walls and traditional Mexican tile flooring. A mural showed a woman dancing to music being played by a gentleman wearing a wide sombrero. Red silk flowers sat in small glass vases at each table.

"I've known Mama since she opened this restaurant twenty-some years ago," said Susie.

"What's this about you helping the local Mexican community?" asked Misty.

"It's nothing big. We use Mexican labor in our business, and I've taken the opportunity to help families get rooted here and elsewhere in this state. It can seem overwhelming to some immigrants, especially with language barriers. I've learned to speak some Spanish. Lily helped me before she got sick."

"That's such a kind thing to do," said Misty, realizing David's generosity came from his mother's example.

"People in Lilac Lake are very caring, for the most part. It's a lesson Rod and I learned from Genie Wittner. She helped Rod and me when we needed it after we first started our business. And we aren't the only ones she's assisted," said Susie.

"She's been a blessing to my sister and me," said Misty, reminding herself to visit GG. Grandmother to the Gilford women, GG loved to be part of their lives and those of their friends.

Their margaritas came.

"Here's to a lovely day," said Susie, raising her glass.

Misty held up her glass, flattered to be sharing time with Susie.

A waiter brought their food to them—an array of small plates that were placed on the table between them.

"Mama has made samples of her favorite dishes. I love this," said Susie. "We can have a taste of a lot of different things."

Misty looked at the food, wondering where to begin. It all looked delicious.

Mama came over to them. "For you, I do special samples. Enjoy."

"We will," said Susie. "Thanks so much."

After eating a fish taco, a sample of a chicken and cheese enchilada, a taste of tamales, and some pozole (hominy soup), Misty was stuffed.

Growing up with Crystal, who was interested in cooking, she'd learned to eat a variety of foods early in her life and was a self-confessed foodie. She was delighted that Susie enjoyed food as much as she did. Misty leaned back against the bench seat and sighed. "That was delicious. Thank you."

"I'd forgotten how much food Mama likes to give her customers. These were just small samples," said Susie.

Mama came over to them. "How was everything?"

"Delicious as usual," said Susie.

"How about some coffee and churros?" said Mama.

Susie turned to Misty. "Are you game?"

Misty chuckled at the idea. "Sure. Why not? I won't have to eat until tomorrow after all of this."

While they waited for dessert to be brought to them, Susie continued to ask Misty questions about her teaching experience in Florida.

"Did you have several students whose first language wasn't English?" Susie asked.

"Several. But children are quick to learn and can speak English fairly quickly at school. The problem was that many spoke only their native tongue at home, which can make it confusing."

"I helped set up a program for adults to learn English in Concord. Our population in the state is slowly changing.

Perhaps you can help in some way."

"Maybe eventually," said Misty. "I need to get established in my job here before I over-commit myself. I'm going to help out at the café for certain events. I'm just not sure how much time I'll have outside of school."

"That's fair. If you find it's something you might be interested in doing, just let me know." Susie smiled at her. "It's satisfying for me to talk about things I used to do. Rod has been after me to get out of the house and be active again. Meeting you has been very helpful. You have the same sort of energy about you that Lily had."

"I'm flattered," said Misty, not willing to tell Susie about her past trauma in Florida. She hoped Lily had never experienced anything like it.

Their dessert came, and though Misty had thought she might be too full to eat anything more, she dug in after the first bite of her churro, which was like a cinnamon doughnut.

When Susie asked for the check, the waiter shook his head firmly. "Mama says it's all taken care of."

Susie sighed. "Please thank her for me. I'll be sure to send people her way."

He bobbed his head and grinned when Susie handed him some folded-up bills for a tip.

As they left the restaurant, Susie placed an arm around Misty and quickly let it drop when Misty stiffened and turned to her.

"I'm sorry," said Misty. "I was surprised. It's fine ... I ..."

"No problem," said Susie. "I like you. I think you know that."

"Yes, I do, and it makes me happy," said Misty. "I realize no one can take the place of Lily, but I do want us to be friends."

"Me, too," said Susie, giving her a knowing look. "We haven't mentioned David, but I'm sure he'd like the idea."

Misty didn't respond, and Susie seemed to understand and talked instead of the Labor Day holiday coming up.

As she climbed into Susie's car, Misty's mind spun. She liked the idea that she and Susie were forming a friendship that wasn't all about David but was more about two women who wanted to support one another.

CHAPTER EIGHT

That afternoon, Misty decided to visit GG at The Woodlands. Genie Wittner had helped Crystal and her throughout the years, had even lent money to Crystal to enable her to open the Lilac Lake Café, and continued to be interested in their wellbeing. Misty thought of her as the only "grandmother" she'd ever had.

Before she drove out of town, Misty stopped at Petals, the cute, green-painted flower shop in town that also sold imported chocolates. GG loved her sweets.

Debbie Sweeney, the owner of the store, greeted Misty. "How are you, young lady? I hear you're going to be my granddaughter's teacher. I'm delighted."

Misty conjured up the list of student names she'd been given. "Oh, yes. Caro Sweeney. I hope she's as excited as I am."

"She's very excited, unlike her older brother, who'd rather play baseball, especially now that Ross Roberts is living in town."

"I understand. It's exciting to think of all the sports opportunities here. Wait until the sports center opens. It's going to be even better than the clinics held at the new baseball field."

"I'm thankful the whole town is behind it," said Debbie. "Now, how can I help you?"

"I need some special chocolates for Ms. Wittner," said Misty.

Smiling, Debbie shook her head. "I swear that woman keeps my store going with all the purchases made for her." She walked behind the counter and pointed to a selection. "These truffles came in this morning. I suggest a mix of flavors."

"Perfect," said Misty. "I'll take a couple of pounds."

"And because it's Genie Wittner, I'll wrap the box for you and add a fresh flower with the bow."

"Thanks," said Misty. "You make everything very nice."

While Misty waited for Debbie to wrap the gift, she looked around. With so many different colorful flowers, it was such a cheerful place.

"Here you go," said Debbie, handing her a box wrapped in silver and tied with a white satin ribbon. A pink rose was tucked into the bow.

"Lovely," said Misty, handing Debbie her credit card. Part of Debbie's success with the shop was her ability to make even the simplest gift or bouquet elegant. She did the flowers for the Inn, all the churches in town, and for many of the weddings and other celebrations, keeping the shop going year-round.

It didn't take long for Misty to drive to The Woodlands. The attractive, one-story stained-brown building had been constructed by Collister Construction, giving Aaron and Brad Collister the credibility they needed to grow their company.

Inside, Misty was told by the receptionist that she could go along and see Ms. Wittner.

Misty walked down the hallway, stopped at GG's apartment, and knocked on the half-open door.

"Come in," called GG.

Misty walked inside and over to where GG was sitting on her couch.

"Good afternoon. I've brought you some treats," Misty said, glad to see GG alert. "I thought you might be taking a nap."

GG gave her a smug look. "I've already had a little cat nap." She patted the cushion next to her. "Please sit."

"This is for you. Debbie Sweeney sent the flower." Misty handed the box to GG and was amused when GG very carefully removed the wrapping.

"Thank you. Everyone knows I love my sweets. This is very thoughtful of you," said GG. She lifted the cover of the box and eyed the truffles inside. "Here. You take one, and then I will."

Not wanting to disappoint her, Misty lifted a chocolate out of the box and waited for GG to choose one.

Then, together, they each took a bite.

"M-m-m," said GG. "Delicious. Now, tell me why you're here on such a nice day."

"I had lunch with Susie Graham. She mentioned your name, and I realized it's been too long since I've seen you. It's always nice to chat with you."

"Susie Graham, huh? My spies tell me you've been seeing David."

Misty chuckled. No one knew exactly how she did it, but GG kept track of everyone in town.

"David and I have gone on a couple of dates. He's very nice. His parents invited me to dinner, and Susie and I hit it off right away. She's lonely after Lily died, and it's been fun to think of her as a mother-type because I didn't have one growing up."

GG clucked her tongue. "It is such a tragedy for the family to lose Lily. I'm glad you've made that connection. Susie is a very special woman. I'm happy for you both."

Misty gripped her hands together, suddenly emotional. "Susie knew my mother when she was about to have me and for a short while afterward. She told me how excited my mother was about me." Tears filled Misty's eyes. "That means so much to me."

GG gave her hand a surprisingly strong grip. "It's important for you to know that. As unorthodox as your upbringing was, there was love before your mother was lost to addiction."

"Everyone in town has always been very kind to Crystal and me," said Misty. "You, especially. I won't ever forget it."

"Just pass it along. That's all I've ever asked of anyone I've ever helped," said GG, smiling at her. "So, tell me about you and David."

Misty shrugged. "There's not much to tell. We've had only a couple of dates. He's a great guy, very caring. I like him a lot." She stared into the distance and turned back to GG. "But it's going to take me a while to get over my memories with Vince. He was such an awful person. Whenever someone touches me unexpectedly, I flinch. I can't help it."

"Do you need to go back to therapy?" GG asked.

"I think it's just going to take time. I worry David will get frustrated with my issues," said Misty honestly.

"You couldn't have chosen a better man than David. He's a gentleman through and through," said GG. "He's always been the one among the kids who knew when to help someone. Growing up, David was instinctively kind."

"Even though he's older and I was the tag-along sister, I remember that about him. So, it makes sense that I can trust David."

GG's blue eyes bore into her. "The more you give yourself chances to get beyond your past, the better off you'll be. But if you need to talk to a professional about it, do it. We can't let anyone ruin your future, can we?"

"No," whispered Misty. *Damn Vince for what he's done. I'll never forgive myself for ignoring the red flags showing what kind of person he was.*

She saw that GG was growing tired and stood. "I'd better go."

GG gave her an encouraging smile. "It's always great to see you. And anytime you need to talk about it, I'm here for you."

Misty leaned down and hugged her. "Thanks. You always know how to make me feel better."

"It's my pleasure to see you," said GG. "No news of Crystal's wedding?"

Misty shook her head. "I know she'd like to elope, but I don't think that's going to happen. But I'm sure you'll be among the first to know when they decide."

GG's eyes sparkled with mischief. "I'm sure I will."

Misty chuckled. "I'll talk to you later. Thanks."

She left GG's apartment and walked through the lobby to the outside. She heard the cry of a cardinal, her lucky bird, and was very satisfied she'd come to see GG.

Misty wasn't surprised when David called her that evening. "Can you talk?"

"Sure. I'm glad you called. I had an amazing time with your mother at lunch. We're both eager to get to know one another better."

"That's nice," he said, and Misty could hear the happiness in his voice. "Do you want to meet at Jake's?"

"Yes, but I'll only have something to drink. I'm still full of lunch at Chica's. I guess it pays to know the owner. Mama Montoya couldn't do enough for your mother."

David chuckled. "They've been friends for a long time. Okay, I'll see you at Jake's. But, Misty, I'd like to take you out to dinner this weekend. Are you up for it?"

"Yes, that would be nice." She didn't care where they went. She just wanted to spend time with him.

CHAPTER NINE

MISTY HEADED TO JAKE'S, EXCITED FOR THE OPPORTUNITY to be with friends. It was such a lovely evening she decided to walk, certain she could get someone to drive her home.

The town was crowded with visitors, but Misty easily wended her way through the sightseers. When she arrived at Jake's, most of the gang was there. Some had already eaten, and others were placing orders. She waited until they were through and ordered a small glass of wine.

As she sat down, David arrived and sat beside her.

JoEllen was telling everyone about the hunky man she saw in the next town when she spent an evening there. "I asked him to stop by. His name is Vince something. You should see his muscles. He makes a lot of guys look like weaklings."

Vince? Misty felt her entire body go numb. Dizzy, she cupped her face in her hands. When she could get her breath, she looked up and found Crystal's worried gaze on her.

Crystal stood. "I'd better go, and I'm taking Misty with me. If that man should appear and ask about either of us, please say nothing. That could be dangerous to us."

David got to his feet. "I'll go with you."

Misty could barely walk away from the table because her

knees were wobbly.

Crystal stopped and turned back. "I'm serious about this, JoEllen. Not a word. Understand? If you do, you'll live to regret it."

"Why is everyone always picking on me?" JoEllen whined.

"Got it?" said Crystal, scowling at JoEllen.

"Okay," said JoEllen. "Guess he's the guy who beat up Misty, huh?"

Crystal didn't bother to answer. She grabbed Misty's arm, and the three of them walked out of the bar.

"Where do you want to go?" David asked, glancing around.

"She can't stay with me," said Crystal. "It won't be safe. He knows I'm her sister. He might try to find her through me." She turned to Misty. "Why don't you go home with David until we're sure the man is not Vince Tucci? I'm on my way to tell Nick about it."

"Maybe it's another Vince. I don't want to bother anyone," said Misty, though her body had grown cold at the thought of seeing him.

"Most likely, it's a different person, but we can't take that chance," Crystal said grimly.

David was quiet during the exchange but now took Misty's arm. "You'll be safe at my cabin. Whoever this guy is, he won't know about it."

"You're right. This may seem silly to you, but as Crystal says, I can't take the chance it could be the Vince I know. My ex, Vince Tucci, has threatened to kill me." Misty choked on her last words.

David's eyes widened. "C'mon, let's get into my truck and get out of here."

"I'll let you know what Nick has to say," said Crystal. "He can talk to JoEllen about the man she met and get a better description."

Misty and David hurried to his truck parked in back of Jake's and took off for his cabin.

As he drove, David's expression was grim. Misty knew how upset he was and noticed that, after they left town, he relaxed his grip on the steering wheel.

He finally spoke. "I'd heard some things about your past when you first returned to Lilac Lake, but I had no idea things were that bad. My God! He threatened to kill you? No wonder Crystal and you are reacting this way. He's a monster."

"She's still trying to keep me safe, like the big sister she's always been," said Misty, shaken by what was happening.

"Rightly so," said David. "Earlier, you told me you had a bad experience in the past. If this is what it was about, it's much more than a bad experience. No matter what went on, I'll help you."

"Thank you," she said, touched to the core.

"Want to talk about it?" David asked in a gentle voice.

"Yes, but I might need a glass of wine to do it," she said, unable to fight off images of Vince's face when he became angry. It was grotesque.

"I teach the kids in my karate class to fight. But it's all done with respect for others until they're forced to defend. It's a fine line between anger and violence, and it's hard for some people to hold back. But once they give in to those impulses, it takes a lot to change them."

David pulled into his driveway and helped her out of his truck. "It's a pleasant night. We can either stay outside on the porch or go inside."

"If you don't mind, I'd feel more comfortable inside," said Misty. Common sense told her she was safe sitting on his porch, but her vivid memories made it seem more secure inside.

Once inside, Misty sat on the couch in the living area.

"What would you like? Red or white wine?" asked David.

"I'd like a glass of red, thank you." Misty hoped it would warm her up. Whenever she thought of Vince being near her, she felt like she were in an old-fashioned nor'easter storm.

David opened a bottle of red wine and brought a glass to her. "I'll grab a beer and be right back."

Misty accepted the wine he offered her and sat back on the couch.

He sat beside her and, giving her a questioning look, took hold of her hand. "Whenever you're ready."

Misty liked the feel of his strong fingers gently placed around her hand. She drew a breath and began. "Vince comes from a wealthy family. They seemed normal at first. Then I began to see how his father dominated everyone and how cruel he could be, and I realized he and Vince had some of the same behaviors. They were never wrong about anything. They had to control all interactions. Everything was on their terms."

"You said Vince's father was domineering. Did you ever see him hit anyone?" asked David.

"No, but he was quick to anger and had an icy stare that could slice you open like a sharp knife," she said, feeling a shudder.

"Vince didn't like it when I turned him down to attend family events. But after I realized his father didn't like me, I couldn't stand the pressure of being with him. Then, the belittling remarks began. They were delivered in a joking matter at first. Things you wouldn't notice right away. Harmless."

"Like what?" David asked.

"When I put on a new dress for a special party, he asked me if that's what I was going to wear, that the color didn't suit me. He told me he'd wait until I changed it. Or sometimes he'd tell me I didn't have time to change clothes to suit him, that I'd have to leave wearing something he said looked awful on me. Then, he started to put down my teaching career, calling me a babysitter. Said I wasn't bright enough to teach high school kids like one of his cousins."

"Typical of some emotional abusers," said David.

Misty took a sip of wine. "I can't tell you some of the other things he said. Thinking of them now makes me sick to my stomach."

David gave her hand a gentle squeeze of encouragement.

"Things got worse when Vince asked me to move in with him. I woke up to what was happening and remembered how my mother was taken in by men who promised her a decent life and how it ruined her and hurt Crystal and me. I knew then there was no way I could live with him. It would've been a nightmare. I knew that all too well from my mother's experiences."

"Did the hitting start then?" asked David.

Misty nodded. "It began with a playful push or a so-called light slap to my back. When Vince smacked me in the face, I told him I wouldn't see him again. He cried and said it would never happen again."

"And it happened again," said David, shaking his head.

"That time, I fought him off, and he went crazy. He'd been drinking all evening, and I knew I was in trouble when he attacked for real. I managed to kick him in his groin, and when I threatened to call the police, he left. Before he could attack again, I grabbed a few things from my apartment, got in the car, and came here."

"So, he knows where you live?" David asked.

"Not exactly. When people asked, I always said I came from the Boston area, not New Hampshire. It sounded a little more glamorous. I didn't realize until after I left how important that might become."

"We'll see what Nick can find out from JoEllen and go from there. Until then, why don't you get comfortable? Would you like to watch a movie?" David's look of concern was endearing. "How about a comedy?

As Misty leaned back, David set up the movie on his TV and took a seat on the couch beside her, leaving plenty of room between them. Something Misty appreciated.

Misty had no idea when she fell asleep, but her eyes fluttered open when David rose and placed a blanket over her. Emotionally spent, she retreated into sleep until memories took over. Then she tossed and turned.

The next morning, she got up and padded to the bathroom. She returned to the couch, wrapped the blanket around her, and went to the front porch to watch the sunrise. It was another hot summer day, and Misty loved observing the early morning activities of the birds and small woodland creatures as they began their day.

She studied the rows of growing trees and bushes and realized how much work David had put into the business. She liked the idea of him growing things. He was such a loving person, and it showed in his work.

At the sound of someone behind her, she turned to see David smiling at her. "It's a nice time of day to sit on the porch. How did you sleep?"

Misty let out a long, worried breath. "After crashing during the movie, I spent a restless night. I just need to know if the man JoEllen saw was Vince Tucci."

"We'll call Nick as soon as we can. For now, how about a cup of coffee?" asked David.

"That would be delightful. Thanks. I take mine with just a touch of milk."

"That's easy. I'll be right back with it."

Misty didn't have to wait long. David quickly returned with coffee for them both and sat in a chair next to hers.

"I've been considering your situation and have two strong suggestions for you," said David. "I think you should enroll in my karate class and learn some valuable defense techniques. I also think you should get a dog. They are a huge protection from someone prowling around."

Misty was quiet. "You're right. I carry a spray on my key chain, but I want more security. I need to learn some karate moves. And I love dogs. I didn't see how I could have one while sharing space with someone. But now I think I can."

"Why don't I help you pick out a dog? And you can start karate lessons with me tomorrow when I'm at the studio."

"Okay. It's a wise idea even if the man JoEllen saw isn't Vince."

"I know someone in the Dog Rescue Program. I'll give him a call in a little while. In the meantime, let's enjoy the sunrise."

As she sat quietly observing her surroundings, Misty realized David was strong, not mean; smart, not foolish; and caring, not self-absorbed. She glanced at him out of the corner of her eye.

He caught her looking at him and smiled, lighting his face,

emphasizing his deep-blue eyes.

Caught in the moment, Misty struggled to find something to say. "Thanks for your help."

His features softened. "Glad to do it."

Misty finished her coffee and went inside to freshen up. She knew Crystal would be awake and called her.

"Morning," Crystal said. "I was just about to call you. Nick phoned to say he talked to JoEllen right after we left Jake's, got a detailed description, and went to the hotel bar where she'd met him. No one by the name of Vince Tucci was staying at the property, and the bartender said the man hadn't been there all evening."

"What about the description? Does it match Vince Tucci?" Misty asked.

"It's hard to say. His name was Vince, but there was no last name. He had black curly hair, eye-color uncertain- maybe hazel, and a broad, muscular build. In today's world, that could mean a lot of different people."

"No noticeable tattoos?" asked Misty, not feeling much better about it.

"He had none that JoEllen remembered. She's not the best witness," said Crystal. "I think she'd had plenty to drink when she saw him."

"Sounds like her," grumped Misty. "David wants to teach me a few karate moves and thinks it's smart for me to get a dog."

"Superb suggestions," said Crystal. "Nick said he'd add

another lock to your front door."

"I guess that's all we can do," said Misty, disheartened. "I'm not on social media, and I have kept any information about me pretty private."

"Everyone in our social group in town is aware of the situation and will keep their vigilance," said Crystal. "For all we know, this person could simply be a regular guy named Vince."

"That's what I have to believe going forward," said Misty. She hated not knowing.

"Have a good day," said Crystal. "Let me know how you do with a dog."

"Okay." Misty was excited to own one.

David came into the house. "Any news?"

"The man JoEllen saw is apparently gone and can't be identified as Vince Tucci. But Crystal likes the idea of karate lessons and my having a dog. She says everyone will keep an eye out for someone looking like Vince Tucci." She shrugged. "I guess that's all I can hope for. Oh, and Nick is putting a stronger lock on my front door."

David studied her. "Okay then. Let's get ready. We'll go to breakfast at the Lilac Lake Café before heading head over to the pet rescue center. Sound like a plan?"

"Yes. I'm anxious to get back to my cabin to take a shower."

"And I need to get to work. I've told the crew I'll be late. They'll go ahead and begin their routines. They know what to do. I'm not worried about them."

###

When they arrived at the café, Nettie hurried over to them. "Misty, I had no idea you had such a difficult experience with your ex-boyfriend. I want you to know I'll post a photo of Vince Tucci by the check-in clock. If my staff see him here, they'll notify the police."

"Thank you," said Misty. "Anything to keep him away from me will help."

"Now, what can I get you two for breakfast? We're trying a new sausage omelet you might like," said Nettie, looking at David.

"Great," said David. "How about you, Misty?"

"I'd like to try a veggie omelet," she said.

"Coming right up," said Nettie, disappearing into the kitchen.

It seemed odd not to see Crystal at the café. She'd been such a part of it for so long. Misty glanced around. The walls had been painted a deeper green, giving it a different feel, but one that would be elegant for the gourmet dinners Crystal and Melissa hoped to put on together occasionally in the café.

While they waited to be served, Misty observed several of her crowd arrive. Dirk came into the café for his usual coffee before heading to his dental office. Taylor came in to work on her book, and Whitney came with her son in a stroller.

Misty was grateful the café remained a favorite hangout with Nettie and Jason running it. She knew how relieved Crystal was to sell it so she and Emmett could marry and create a family.

Their food arrived, and they ate in privacy.

David's cell rang, and he answered the call. "Hi, Gage. Did you get my message? Okay, Misty and I will be there in a while. Thanks." He ended the call and turned to her. "Gage Martens, who acts as a vet for the Animal Rescue Center, thinks he might have the ideal dog for you."

"How exciting! I can't wait to see it. No matter what, the dog and I must have a special connection, or it won't work."

"Absolutely," said David.

They each paid as soon as they finished, and then the two of them left.

The Animal Rescue Center was in a one-story brick building outside of town. Tucked under the shade of a large maple tree, the building had a large fenced-in area beside it where a few dogs were sitting, lying down, or playing. Seeing David and Misty, a few of them began to bark.

Inside, a young man with straight brown hair and butterscotch eyes looked up from behind the desk where he was signing papers. " 'Morning, David. And this must be Misty."

"Hello," said Misty.

David introduced him to Misty. "This is Gage Martens, the new vet here."

"I'm a recent addition to the area and haven't met many

people socially yet. David and I are planning to join up at Jake's tonight so I can meet y'all," Gage said with a southern twang.

"Are you from the south?" she asked. "A new friend living here is from outside New Orleans."

"I'm from Virginia," said Gage. He stood, and Misty realized he was taller than she'd thought. "Now, what can we do for you? I understand you're interested in a dog that would serve as a guard dog. I have a couple in mind."

"Before you show me, can I just look at all the available ones?" Misty asked.

"Certainly. Follow me," said Gage.

He led them into a room lined with built-in cages on two of the walls.

"We have cats in a separate section. Every dog here is available for adoption," Gage explained. "If you see one you're interested in, we'll take the dog out of its cage so you can interact with it."

Misty noticed the carpet in the middle of the room where several toys lay and realized the purpose of the play area.

Taking a deep breath, Misty walked slowly by the cages, looking at each dog. Their hopeful expressions or looks of resignation touched her. She passed several large dogs who would, no doubt, be suitable.

Then, her glance met the brown eyes belonging to a small, curly-haired, tan dog whose pointed nose looked as if she had a bit of Dachshund in her, along with a curly-haired breed, maybe a Poodle. The dog wagged its tail, and Misty couldn't help smiling. "How about this one?"

Gage frowned. "She's sweet, but I'm not sure what kind of guard dog she'd make. She likes everyone."

"I'd like the chance to play with her. What is her name?" asked Misty.

"Sugar," said Gage. He indicated a big chocolate lab. "Now, Duke here would be a better choice."

"No," insisted Misty. "I want to see Sugar."

Gage opened the cage, and Sugar immediately went into Misty's arms and kissed her cheeks. Giggling, Misty stroked her head and then took a deep, long look into the dog's round, brown eyes.

"Will you protect me, Sugar?" she said softly, and Sugar barked and looked around, alert.

"Tell me about her," Misty said to Gage.

"She's about four years old, was the only dog of a woman who had to move into an assisted living facility, and she's a trained therapy dog. We just got her, so she hasn't been listed for adoption. That's why she's still here. She's a great dog, but I thought you needed one that was bigger, more likely to defend you," said Gage.

"She's very alert. She can let me know if something is wrong," said Misty. "I'm much more comfortable with her." She got to her feet and said, "Come." Sugar followed her around the room. Misty knelt, and Sugar went right up to her and kissed her cheek.

"She's perfect," said Misty, standing. "I want her."

"Okay, we'll discuss your home and surroundings, and then we'll fill out the paperwork. I have her medical records. You can see she's in excellent health. She's trim and has had all her shots."

Gage put a leash on Sugar and handed it to Misty.

On the way out of the room, Misty kept her eyes on the floor. She couldn't bear to see the dogs left behind.

Gage handed her some paperwork, and they went over it together. "If you don't think it will work out for any reason, you have three days to change your mind. You understand that could be traumatic for the dog, but we want to be sure the placement is satisfactory for you both."

Misty completed the paperwork, paid the fees, and then turned to David. "Isn't she wonderful?"

David grinned. "It's a love match all right."

Misty laughed and picked up Sugar, who fit comfortably into her arms. "Good girl, Sugar. We're going home."

CHAPTER TEN

David dropped Misty and Sugar off at her cabin and helped her carry in the dog bed, toys, and food the previous owner had given the Animal Rescue Center for Sugar. There wasn't a doubt in Misty's mind that the dog was well-loved. As soon as things got calmer, she intended to take Sugar to see her former owner. It was the least she could do. She'd learned Sugar's former owner, a woman named Cassandra Overton, lived at The Woodlands.

Misty allowed Sugar to sniff all around the cabin. When she was through, Misty opened the sliding glass door and took her out onto the deck.

"I know the woods are exciting, but you must stay with me for now. We'll walk together later," said Misty.

Sugar looked up at her and wagged her tail.

Misty leaned over and rubbed her ears. "You really are a sweet dog."

Inside, Misty took off the dog's leash, carried the dog's bed to a corner of the kitchen, and set it down. It would allow Sugar to sleep in the sunshine sometimes, and from there, Sugar would have a view of both the front door and the sliding glass door. Sugar went over to it, sniffed it, and turned in circles three times before lying down in it.

"Good girl," said Misty. "This is your new home."

She heard a sound at the front door.

Sugar barked, ran to the door, and stood by, alert and cautious.

"Okay. Let's see who's visiting," said Misty. She opened the door and found Crystal standing there. "Hi. Are you here to see my new dog?"

"Yes. I'm curious to see if she's going to work out. I hear she's cute."

Misty stood back to allow Crystal inside.

The dog looked at Misty. "It's okay," she said.

Only then, wagging her tail, did Sugar allow Crystal to touch her.

"Wow, she's beautifully trained," said Crystal patting Sugar.

"She's a therapy dog. Her previous owner is a new resident at The Woodlands from Portsmouth. I'm told she's glad that Sugar will remain close by."

"Well, she's adorable. But I'm also here to find out how you're doing. The thought of Vince being nearby was scary. I just came from seeing Nick at the police station. He doesn't think the man JoEllen saw was Vince Tucci, but he says this is a wake-up call to all of us. We must be vigilant for one another.

"Learning about 'stranger danger' is important for kids of all ages old enough to understand," said Misty. "Maybe Sugar can help in some way."

"That's a great idea," said Crystal. "I know Emmett kccps a little booklet about the need to be careful with strangers for patients at his office."

"Can you stay for a cup of coffee or some lemonade?" Misty asked.

"Thanks. I'd like to," said Crystal. "I haven't been here since you first moved in. You've decorated it very nicely. It's a wonderful spot."

"Yes, it's perfect for me. And after this scare, I'm grateful to have other cabins around. It makes it seem safer," said Misty, leading her sister into the kitchen.

Crystal studied her. "Do you want to make more appointments with your counselor to talk about the trauma?"

"No, my counselor and I discussed the work I need to do for myself. But I'm excited that David is going to teach me some defensive karate moves."

She handed Crystal a glass of lemonade and fixed one for herself. "Let's go outside. I want to see what Sugar does about staying close to the house."

They went out to the deck and sat in chairs facing one another.

"David is a great guy. I'm happy you trust him," Crystal told her.

"I do trust him. He's a special man. He was a great comfort to his sister through the months she was dying. He says they had a sibling relationship a lot like ours, with his sister keeping an eye on him."

"He comes from a lovely family. I didn't get to know his mother very well. I can't imagine how much she missed her daughter. I think it's nice that you and she have a growing relationship."

"That, and her connection to my birth makes it important to me. Susie was there when I was born, and that means a lot to me, especially when she tells me I was loved." Misty felt a knot in her throat and stopped talking.

Crystal reached out a hand to her, and Misty took it. "You've always been loved," Crystal said softly.

"I know," Misty said. "You made sure of it. I'm eternally grateful to you."

"How is the preparation for school going?" Crystal asked, changing the subject just as Sugar began barking.

A squirrel scrambled up the trunk of a tree while Sugar watched helplessly. Misty and Crystal laughed at the scene.

"Guess she's going to keep me safe from squirrels," said Misty. "So far, she's staying pretty close. When I eventually talk to her previous owner, I intend to ask her all sorts of questions about the dog."

"Nice for both of you that you'll be able to do that," said Crystal. Smiling, she leaned forward and grinned at Misty. "I have a question for you. Emmett and I are talking about a surprise wedding over Labor Day. Something small and intimate at Emmett's house. Will you be my maid of honor?"

"Yes! I'm very honored. But what do you mean 'surprise wedding'?"

"We would let just a few people know ahead of timc. Otherwise, we'll announce a picnic at his house. The surprise is mostly for his parents. As a senator, his father wants a showy wedding. His mother would prefer a quiet one with no alcohol. We're doing our best to do what we want for ourselves without hurting anyone else. What do you think?"

"I believe you should have the wedding of your dreams, and if that's a small, intimate one with a picnic reception, it'll be perfect. Emmett has purposely stayed out of his father's political life, and you've both helped his mother with her addiction issues. You deserve to have the ceremony you want."

Crystal clasped her hands with a joyful expression. "Okay, then. Emmett is going to ask Nick to be his best man. I'll wear a simple white dress. You can choose any summer dress you want, but I think a floral pattern would be nice."

"Excellent!" Misty got up and hugged her sister.

Sugar saw them, bounded over, and growled until Misty said, "It's okay, girl."

The dog backed away and then came to Misty's side.

Crystal shook her head with amazement. "She's protecting you. I'm very impressed."

Misty picked up the dog and hugged it to her. "She and I chose one another. She's perfect for me."

They walked Crystal to the front door.

"See you later," said Misty. "I'm going into town for a certain dress I saw at the Wild Flower Boutique. I normally allow myself only to look at all her beautiful clothing, but I'm going to splurge for such a happy occasion."

"Poppy Browning has such excellent, fun taste. No matter what it is, it'll be fabulous," said Crystal. She beamed at her. "I'm getting excited. Thanks, sis."

"Thank you for asking me," Misty replied, fighting tears. She loved Crystal so much.

That afternoon, Misty decided to do a test run in town with her new dog. She didn't want to leave Sugar home while she went looking for a dress, and taking Sugar with her would be a smart way to introduce the dog to the area. The small town was very dog-friendly.

She put Sugar's leash on and told her they were going for a ride. The dog responded with a lot of tail wagging and tugging on her leash, anxious to leave.

"You understand what I'm saying," Misty said, laughing. "Okay, then, you can help me choose a dress."

Downtown, Misty got Sugar out of the car and headed to the Wild Flower Boutique. Painted yellow, the store front was attractive, with sunflowers in tall brown pots beside the steps into the shop. Hopefully, the dress she'd seen earlier was still there. And if she was very, very lucky, it might be on sale.

She was excited by the thought of seeing Poppy, who was in her late 30s and was always a pleasure to talk to. Though she kept up on what was going on in town, she wasn't a gossip, and she was friendly to everyone.

Misty led Sugar to the door and paused. "Poppy, is it all right if I bring my new dog into your store? She's very well-behaved."

Poppy looked up from behind the jewelry counter. "Of course. What a cute dog." She headed toward them. Not trim, Poppy was a brunette who had chocolate brown eyes and a ready smile.

Holding out her hand, Poppy bent to greet Sugar, who wiggled with pleasure at the attention. "What's your name, sweet dog?" Poppy cooed.

"This is Sugar. I got her this morning. She's a trained therapy dog and a real sweetheart," Misty said proudly. "Her former owner is at The Woodlands."

"Oh, how nice. Will you take Sugar to see her from time to time?" Poppy asked, straightening.

"That's my plan," said Misty. "I don't know much about the woman except she had to find a home for Sugar."

"Are you browsing today?" asked Poppy, and Misty couldn't help smiling. Browsing was all she usually did.

"I'm here to find a sundress. I saw one here a couple of weeks ago that I liked. I'm hoping you still have it."

"I've put some in the back. Let's go check." Poppy led her to the back of the store, where a rack of clothes was marked on sale.

"Oh, I don't see it. The dress was white with bright, colorful flowers. Simple but sweet," said Misty.

"I think I know which one you meant. It's gone. But let me

show you something similar. It's in a pale pink that would look great on you."

Poppy left her and returned with a simple A-line style dress with a V-neck and capped sleeves. Misty knew it would be perfect.

"Let me try it on. Hopefully, it'll fit. I love it," gushed Misty.

After she slipped it on, Misty studied herself in the mirror. As she'd thought, it would be fine with any color scheme Crystal chose for her wedding.

She stepped out of the dressing room to show Poppy.

Poppy studied her thoughtfully and grinned. "It's lovely on you. I was going to show you another if this one didn't work, but after seeing you in this, I'm not going to suggest it."

Misty looked at Sugar. "Do you like it?"

Sugar barked once, twice.

"Okay, I'll take it," said Misty. She held back a gulp of worry at the price.

Poppy seemed to notice. "How about I put this on sale for you? It's been here a few weeks, and I have to think of making room for fall clothes."

Misty gave Poppy a wide smile. "Thank you."

"Is this for a special occasion?" Poppy asked a few minutes later as she carefully folded the dress in tissue.

"Just an end-of-summer treat," said Misty. "Of course, anything from your store is a treat. You have the nicest things. Your taste is excellent."

Poppy chuckled. "I buy all the things I'd want for myself. Is anything special planned in town for Labor Day? I wasn't able to join because I had to take care of my mother. But now that she's gone, I've decided to participate more in local events."

"In that case, why don't you come to Jake's in the evenings? That's where a lot of us locals hang out for drinks and/or supper and conversation. Most everyone is busy, but it's a nice way to connect with others. Are you living alone now?"

Looking sad, Poppy nodded. "It's time for me to get back into the swing of things. I moved here to take care of my mother and decided to open the store."

"Okay. Why don't you meet me and the others at Jake's at seven? We'll be at our usual table in the back. You never know who'll show up, but it's always good to be together."

"Thanks," said Poppy. "I'll do that."

Misty left the store excited about her purchase and a chance to include Poppy, who'd done her such a nice favor.

CHAPTER ELEVEN

THAT EVENING, DAVID CAME TO HER HOUSE.

Sugar looked from her to David and then stepped forward as Misty opened the door.

"Hi. I stopped by to see how the two of you are doing together. Gage said there was some leeway if you decided the adoption wasn't going to work out." He bent and stroked Sugar's ears.

"It's been wonderful having Sugar here. She's such great company. And she's going to work out well as a guard dog of sorts. Even now, you saw how cautious she was before welcoming you. She did the same thing with Crystal."

"Oh, good dog," said David. He looked up at Misty. "Are you going to Jake's tonight?"

"Yes," she answered. "I've invited Poppy Browning from the Wild Flower Boutique to join us. Gage will be there, and it'll be nice for both of them to be introduced to the gang."

"Do you want to go there together?"

Misty shook her head. "No, thanks. I'm going to stay just long enough to test Sugar being alone in the house. This is new to her, and I need to know she's comfortable."

"Okay," he said. "See you later. I've got to go home and

clean up from work. I'll meet you at Jake's."

"Thanks for checking on us," said Misty. "I like having you do that."

"I know," he said, and after giving Sugar a last pat on the head, he left.

Misty watched him go, wishing she was in a different place emotionally. She'd felt the sexual attraction between them for months now, but memories of her time with Vince were sending her reeling backward. She couldn't lose control of her life because of a man again. Misty looked down at Sugar, whose brown eyes were studying her. "I'm glad you're here," she said, stroking Sugar's curly head.

When Misty walked into Jake's that evening, she was pleased to see that Poppy was already there.

Misty went right over to her. "I'm delighted you made it. Have you met everyone?" At Poppy's nod, Misty continued. "David is coming with Gage Martens, the new vet in town. I met him this morning, and he seems very nice."

"Heard you got a dog," said Brad Collister. "What kind of guard dog is named Sugar?" he teased.

"She's smart and protective," said Misty. "I'm lucky to have found her."

"Brad's just teasing. You should see Brad with my dog, Pirate," said Dani. "Talk about a doting dad."

Everyone laughed at the sheepish expression that crossed

Brad's face.

"Is the new vet single?" asked JoEllen.

"I'm pretty sure he is," Misty responded.

Just then, David walked in with Gage.

David approached the table and introduced Gage to everyone there.

After they sat down, Gage turned to Aaron Collister, who owned Collister Construction with his half-brother, Brad. "I understand you're very talented with animals and that people call on you sometimes to help them with behavior problems."

"He's like an animal whisperer," said Crystal, smiling at Aaron.

Aaron studied Gage. "Why do you ask?"

"I have a dog at the Animal Rescue Center who needs some individual work. I'm sure she's been abused, but I don't want to give up on her."

"I'll stop by," said Aaron.

Misty listened to the exchange with interest. Aaron had a quiet, calming assurance about him. Aaron's Native American mother, from the Abenaki tribe, was a healer before she died, and Aaron was left with Brad's family.

JoEllen beamed at Gage. "I hear a Southern accent. Where are you from?"

"Virginia," Gage said. "And you?"

"I'm from the Midwest, but I feel like a native of this town after my sister married Brad. I came to visit them often before she died," said JoEllen.

Gage looked from her to Brad.

"I've since married Dani," said Brad, putting an arm around her.

Misty knew from the tense way Brad spoke that JoEllen had touched a nerve as she often did when conversing with someone in the group.

"How's the dog?" Gage asked Misty.

She felt a huge smile cross her face. "It's a perfect match. I'm not staying too much longer. I'm testing to see how Sugar does with being left alone in my house."

"Even if she misses you, it's good for her to be there alone, to think of it as her place to protect," said Gage.

Misty felt herself relax.

Emmett arrived with Crystal. Everyone moved to make room for them at one of the tables.

"How is everyone?" Emmett asked. "It's my night off, so I can relax." He spoke to Misty. "I hear you got a dog to protect you."

"Yes, she's a sweetie. Very alert, very attentive," said Misty. She opened her phone and passed a photo of Sugar around.

Amid all the positive comments, Crystal said, "It's important, everyone, to keep an eye on one another. This town has always been known for that. It's something we don't want to lose even as the town continues to grow."

"Yeah, at first it was annoying, but I get it," said Cooper, a literary agent married to Taylor. Though they lived most of the year in New York City, they'd grown to love their time in Lilac Lake.

"Where are you living?" Whitney asked Gage.

"Just outside of town. On a piece of property near the Collister's Farm Stand. The house needs some work, but I have some acreage and a small barn, which is nice for the two horses I have."

"Oh, I love cowboys," said JoEllen, and many at the two tables for locals rolled their eyes.

Misty noticed the look of amusement on Gage's face and realized he already understood what kind of person JoEllen was. He caught her eye and winked.

Sitting across from her, David grinned at them, and she felt its warmth.

Much of the following conversation was learning about Poppy and Gage. Listening to them talk about their reasons for coming to Lilac Lake, Misty realized how important it was to add new people to the mix. It kept relationships from getting stale, and it helped keep a sense of community.

Misty stayed long enough to have a beer and a salad and then excused herself. "Sorry, but I have to get back home to check on Sugar. I don't want to leave her for too long. Nice to see everyone and to have Poppy and Gage join us."

David stood. "I'll walk you to your car."

"Thanks," said Misty. Of them all, David was the one person who knew how scared she'd been at the thought of seeing her ex-boyfriend.

Outside the bar, Misty turned to David. "I appreciate all you've done for me. I'm very thankful for Sugar and feel much better about things."

"Don't forget. You promised me you would take a couple of karate lessons. I teach at Kung Fu Karate, which is run by the regional high school. I'm an instructor tomorrow night. I think you should come and observe a couple of classes. Then I can arrange to teach you on your own."

"Okay. I'll do it. I'll feel better knowing I can defend myself."

"It's important." David looked down and shuffled his feet. When he lifted his gaze to her, she noted a flicker of sadness and wondered if she'd imagined it.

"I was small for my age and bullied by one kid in school who moved away in the eighth grade," he said. "But for a year, he made my life miserable. That's when my parents signed me up for karate lessons. It changed my life. I was never bullied again."

"You're very tall now," said Misty, studying his trim but muscular frame.

He chuckled. "It surprised us all when the growth spurt happened suddenly. I went from being one of the shortest kids in class to one of the tallest."

She studied him for a moment. "You're always trying to help me. I appreciate it."

He put a hand on her shoulder. "You're a strong woman. You've had a horrible experience and are doing your best to rebuild your life..." his voice drifted off.

Misty had the feeling he wanted to say more, but he

remained silent.

He leaned down and quickly kissed her cheek, leaving behind a fluttering sensation inside her.

As he walked away, she realized she hadn't pulled away from him and lifted a hand to touch her cheek.

Misty went to the front door of her house to unlock it, curious to see what she'd find inside. She could hear Sugar barking. Smiling at the fierceness of it, Misty opened the door and then laughed as the dog lunged for her with enthusiastic cries of joy.

Misty set down her purse and lifted the dog into her arms, giggling as Sugar covered her cheeks with kisses.

"Aw, sweetie, I missed you too," Misty murmured, thrilled by the dog's response to her.

"And good dog for barking. You sounded like a big, ferocious guard dog, not the softie you are."

Misty set the dog down. Closing the door behind her, she went into her living room, pleased to see everything in order. "I don't know what Cassandra Overton did to train you so well, but I can't wait to thank her in person," she said to Sugar. "I'll call tomorrow morning to make an appointment for us to see her."

Sugar looked up at her and wagged her tail as Misty picked up her leash.

Misty got ready for bed after taking Sugar for a walk in the neighborhood, allowing her to sniff a lot and become accustomed to her new surroundings.

She was surprised when Sugar jumped up on her bed, laid her head on one of the pillows, and curled up with contentment.

"So, that's how it is, huh?" There was no question about where Sugar intended to sleep, and it was all right with Misty.

Misty got up and dressed for her usual walk. This morning, she'd show Sugar her normal route. They'd have to change the routine as soon as school started, but until then, she'd stick to her summer one.

As they headed out of the house, Misty observed Sugar's calm behavior on her leash and was thrilled by the idea of having the dog accompany her. Lilac Lake didn't have a lot of crime, but the thought of Vince finding her had become a real possibility in her mind.

Walking down the street, Misty waved to a few people who drove by and headed for the park David's family had created.

When she entered it, she saw David's mother talking to an elderly gentleman. Unwilling to disturb her, she walked by them and took a seat on a bench in the back corner.

Sugar sat peacefully at Misty's feet and then lay down.

Misty drew in deep breaths and closed her eyes, feeling her body relax as she breathed in the sweet smell of the flowers.

When she sensed someone nearby, Misty's eyes flashed

open.

"'Morning," said David's mother. "It's nice to see you."

Misty smiled at her. "Hi, Susie. How are you?"

"I'm good. Mind if I sit down? I want to see this lovely dog. David has raved about her."

"Meet Sugar," said Misty with a note of possessiveness and pride that surprised her.

Sugar sat by, wagging her tail as Susie stroked her ears. "She's lovely," Susie said to Misty. "I heard about the scare you had. I understand you went to David's cabin, but if you need a place to stay for longer, you're always welcome at my house."

"Thanks. David is going to teach me some karate moves, and between that and having Sugar to help protect me, I'm hoping I won't ever need to take you up on your offer."

Susie gave her a long look. "Physical and emotional abuse can take a toll on a person. Don't be afraid to reach out and talk to someone about it. I grew up with an abusive father until my mother divorced him. That's how I got into nursing and social work."

"Thanks. I talked to Roberta Humphreys after I first returned to town. She's been helpful," said Misty. "I'm working on some exercises she suggested, and it might be helpful to talk to you about them."

"I'd be delighted. Roberta has an excellent reputation," said Susie, still stroking the dog's ears. "Time is flying by. You must be anxious to start school."

"Yes, it'll be exciting to meet all my students. We're in

school for a couple of days before the Labor Day weekend, and then we resume our full schedule."

"I don't mean to sound presumptuous, but I have a few things of Lily's that I thought you might be able to use. Clothing and other items. You and she are about the same size, and it would make me happy to put them to use."

"That's very sweet of you. I'd be glad to look and see if there's anything I can use," said Misty, touched by Susie's thoughtfulness.

Susie beamed at her. "Fine. I'm available anytime tomorrow if you're able to come to the house. Let me know what time works for you."

"Tomorrow afternoon is perfect," said Misty. "Shall we say two o'clock?"

"Yes, thank you." Susie took hold of Misty's hand and squeezed it before she stood. "You're welcome to bring Sugar."

"Okay, thanks." Misty studied her as Susie made her way through the park, stopping to pick weeds from a flower bed before going on her way.

Misty treasured their friendship.

CHAPTER TWELVE

Later, after introducing Sugar to the people at the Café and grabbing a cup of coffee, Misty headed home. She'd had Sugar for only one day but felt her horizons expanding with her presence. People she scarcely knew stopped to talk to her and pet the dog. Pro that she was, Sugar took the attention in stride.

At home, Misty showered and dressed for the day, then called The Woodlands to speak to Cassandra Overton to see about Sugar visiting her.

"I'm sorry, Ms. Overton isn't able to talk to anyone. But I know she'd love to see her pet. Why don't you come ahead with her dog? I'll see that Ms. Overton is prepared. Just come to the front desk, and I'll take you to see her."

"Okay, I'll do that," Misty said, confused by the need for Sugar's owner to be prepared. She put a leash on the dog, put her in her car, and drove to The Woodlands.

The handsome, one-story wooden building sat in a woodsy area outside of town and spread across land well-maintained by Graham Landscaping.

Sugar seemed to sense something exciting. When Misty parked the car and opened the door, Sugar jumped out of the backseat and tugged on her leash to get inside.

At the front desk, Misty explained who she was. A nurse emerged from the nearby office and introduced herself. "You're here to see Ms. Overton, right?"

Misty nodded as Sugar wagged her tail.

"Ms. Overton is in the Memory Care Wing, which is why I wanted to accompany you for the visit. She has good days and bad days."

"But she only recently came here," said Misty, confused. "Unless someone else was taking care of the dog."

"Her niece has been caring for both Ms. Overton and Sugar until recently, but she recognized that both needed more permanent help."

"I see," said Misty. "Will she recognize Sugar?"

The nurse smiled and glanced at Sugar. "I'm almost certain she will. Dogs make such an endearing impression on most of our patients. Let's go see, shall we?"

Misty followed the nurse to a discreet hallway unseen from the reception area.

The nurse opened a heavy wooden door and led Misty and Sugar down another corridor to a private room.

Standing by the open doorway, the nurse called softly to Cassandra Overton. "Ms. Overton? We have some special guests here to see you." The nurse waved Misty and Sugar inside.

In her excitement, Sugar tugged on her leash. Misty dropped it, allowing Sugar to go to her former owner. With tears in her eyes, Misty watched a woman who had been sitting statue-like come to life.

"Doggie!" Ms. Overton exclaimed, smiling.

Misty walked over to Ms. Overton and knelt beside her. "This is Sugar. Remember her?"

Light blue eyes studied her and then returned to Sugar, who'd laid her head in Ms. Overton's lap. When she looked at Misty again, Ms. Overton's eyes overflowed with tears. Seeming to understand who she was, Ms. Overton patted Sugar. "Good dog. Sweet as sugar."

Sugar stretched her paws onto Ms. Overton's lap and licked the tears off her cheeks.

Unable to stop tears from stinging her eyes, Misty took hold of Ms. Overton's hand. "I promise to take care of Sugar."

Ms. Overton turned to Misty, and for a moment, it was as if the older woman's expression livened before the spirit behind it disappeared again.

Misty stood and picked up Sugar, who was softly whimpering. "It's all right, Sugar, we'll come back. Come with me."

Blinded by tears, Misty set the dog down and led her away.

The nurse caught up with them. "Thank you for visiting her. I'm sure Ms. Overton enjoyed seeing her dog. Obviously, the two of them were close."

"I'll try to bring Sugar back to visit her again," said Misty. "Sugar loved it too."

They returned to the reception area.

Thinking of GG, Misty said to the woman manning the reception desk, "While I'm here, I'm wondering if I can visit with Ms. Wittner."

"Of course. Do you know her room number?"

"Yes," said Misty, relieved to have a reason to smile after the sadness she'd felt with Ms. Overton. "Everyone in town knows where GG lives."

"She's our most popular resident," admitted the woman. "Go along. And, if you're willing, please spend a few minutes with the residents in the living room before you leave."

"I'd be happy to. Sugar is a trained therapy dog," said Misty.

Misty led Sugar down the hallway to GG's room. She knocked and, hearing GG's response, entered her apartment.

"Oh, my! It's you, Misty, and your adorable dog. I've heard all about her," said GG, beaming at them both.

Misty chuckled. GG had a network of sources better than anyone she knew.

GG cooed and stroked Sugar's ears and turned to Misty. "How about some lemonade?"

"Thanks. I'd love some. May I fix a glass for you?"

"That would be lovely, dear," said GG. "Then sit and talk to me."

Misty poured each of them a glass of lemonade from the pitcher in the refrigerator and brought them to the living room. She handed one to GG sitting on the couch, and then sat in a chair opposite her. She was amused to see Sugar lying by GG's feet. The dog knew how to make herself comfortable.

GG took a sip of lemonade and faced Misty. "I understand you had a bit of a scare the other night."

Misty told her about staying at David's house and how his mother had offered to let her stay at her house whenever she needed to. She also told her that Susie was offering her some of Lily's things.

"The Grahams are a lovely family," said GG. "Susie is someone who does things for other people without a lot of fanfare. I know how heartbroken the family is to have lost Lily, and I think it's sweet of you to spend some time with Susie. It's an excellent way to help her."

"I'm happy to do it. Having her tell me about my mother has been a gift to me. Are you going to come to town for any of the Labor Day Weekend Celebrations?"

A twinkle entered GG's eyes. "Well, I've been invited to a very private celebration that only a few people, including you, know about."

Misty clasped her hands. "The wedding! I'm so excited! Crystal and Emmett are so wonderful together. Wait until you see my dress. Poppy at the Wild Flower Boutique picked it out for me. It's perfect."

"How is Poppy doing? I remember when she first opened the store. She was concerned about getting year-round support, but I understand she's done really well with it."

"She seems to be busy. And she's now occasionally meeting the rest of us at Jake's. And Gage Martens, the new vet in town, has joined us too."

"It's nice to see the 'summer group' grow and expand with many new professionals in town," said GG. "It means they're likely to remain here." She gave Misty a steady look. "How about you? I understand you're starting to teach in a few days. I'm delighted you'll be teaching at Emerson Wittner Elementary School. It seems right to have you be a part of the family, so to speak. I'm sure my father would be pleased."

"Thank you. I'm honored," said Misty, blinking rapidly. She checked her watch. "It's been nice chatting with you, GG, but I'd better go. We're going to visit residents in the living room. Then I need to have lunch and go see Susie. This evening, I'm going to a karate class that David teaches. At his suggestion, I'll be taking private lessons from him."

"That sounds like a good idea," said GG, giving her a wide smile.

Misty gave GG a kiss on the cheek, waved goodbye, and left, her emotions still reeling from her visit with Cassandra Overton.

At home, Misty decided to go through her clothes. She looked forward to having some new pieces but didn't want to abuse Susie's generosity. She'd take only what she needed. It didn't bother her that the clothes were secondhand. She and her BFF in Florida had loved to go thrifting for clothes. This would be much better because the items would have a special meaning.

Misty ate a light lunch, put a leash on Sugar, and took off for Susie's house. She was enjoying her growing friendship with David's mother but didn't want her or anyone else to automatically assume that she and David were together. Misty wasn't ready to think in those terms.

Misty pulled into the driveway of David's parents' house. She got out of the car and took a moment to study her surroundings. The house was something she'd admired from her previous visit. It sat in a beautiful setting where the lawn met evergreen and deciduous trees. The lake sparkled in the sun at the bottom of the rise of land where the house stood.

The house seemed to greet her as warmly as Susie, who'd opened the back entrance and was walking toward her.

"Hi, right on time," said Susie, smiling at her.

Misty waved and let Sugar out of the car. "I brought her as you suggested." She unhooked the dog from her leash. It's okay, girl, go run and play," said Misty, and Sugar took off running for the lake.

"Come on inside. I've set out a few things for you to look at, but there's much more. I've kept most of Lily's things, but now it's time for them to go to a new home."

Feeling Susie's warmth and hearing such sadness in her voice, Misty turned to her. "If this is too early, too difficult, we don't have to do this."

"Oh, that's sweet of you, but I hope this will be good for both of us."

They walked into the living room and out to the sunporch to check on Sugar. Nose to the ground, Sugar was sniffing the rocks and gravel by the water.

"She probably smells the ducks," said Susie. "Are you comfortable leaving her there?"

"Yes. It looks like she's having fun."

"Okay, then, let's go up to Lily's room. As I've said, I've laid out some things."

They climbed the stairs and went to a bedroom whose walls were painted a pretty lavender.

"Eventually, I'll repaint this room and fix it up as a guestroom," said Susie. "It has a lovely view."

Misty walked over to the window and looked outside. Sugar sprawled in the sun on the dock. Smiling, she turned to Susie. "This is a great place for a dog."

"I think we're ready," said Susie. "I understand we have a new vet at the Animal Rescue Center. I plan to talk to him about it."

"He's very nice," said Misty, standing by the queen-sized bed.

"The clothing lying there are items that I think suit you."

Misty lifted one of the sweaters Susie had placed there. It was a gray, Irish-style sweater. "This is beautiful."

"Try it on. It should fit you. You're about Lily's size." Susie picked up another sweater, a bright blue one. "This was one of her favorites. It'll look beautiful on you."

Misty tried on the sweaters and then some skirts, dresses, slacks, and tops that Susie brought out. The more she tried on, the more excited Susie became.

"It does my heart good to know you're willing to put them to use," said Susie. "Lily would've loved getting to know you."

"It's very kind of you," said Misty. "The things you've chosen for me are beautiful, items I might not be able to afford on my own. Thank you." She glanced at the pile of clothes that had quickly grown.

"You're welcome to go through her closet, but we've chosen the nicest ones," said Susie.

"This is plenty," said Misty. The thought of going through Lily's closet was eerie to her. She glanced at the framed photo on top of the white dresser. It was a picture of a lovely blond woman and David, taken before Lily's illness. Lily and David looked surprisingly alike. Misty knew she could never take Lily's place, but she also knew what a comfort she was to David's mother.

Susie held out a large plastic bag. "We can put the clothes in here." They folded and placed the clothes in the bag, and then Susie let out a long sigh. "That's a big load off my mind. Thank you, Misty."

"I should be thanking you." Misty reached out and clasped Susie's hand. She searched for more adequate words but was suddenly overcome by the sadness of it all.

Understanding, Susie came over to her, and the two

hugged each other silently, letting thc momcnt say what was in their heart.

After stowing the bag in her car, Misty returned to the house. Susie offered her a glass of iced tea, and they each took a glass to the sun porch. "I wonder what's going on at the Lilac Lake Inn," said Susie. "It looks like a wedding."

They sat and watched from a distance as a ceremony was taking place on the Inn's grassy front lawn.

Misty thought of Crystal's wedding and could hardly wait. The wedding might be small, but she knew it would be lovely. If only Emmett's family would cooperate.

She hesitated, then said to Susie, "I appreciate what you've told me about my mother and your experience in social work and need to talk to you. I've been trying to deal with the aftermath of being in an abusive situation. I'm learning to say no when I don't feel comfortable being with someone or don't want to do something."

"And how does that make you feel?" Susie asked.

"More in control. But I need to be careful about not hurting anyone," said Misty. She didn't want to mention David's name.

Susie took hold of her hand and looked her in the eye. "We all have the right to our own space, so not inviting anyone into it is all right. And we all can choose how we want to live. But that doesn't mean we might not need to compromise on how best to move forward without infringing on others' rights."

Misty let out a long breath. "I remember the awful things my ex-boyfriend said to hurt me. I wanted to fight against his words, but that just made him angry. And he wouldn't let me walk away. He always had the last say."

"Are you learning to speak up for yourself?" asked Susie gently.

"Yes, I am. But I struggle sometimes. And when I feel frustrated, I tend to clam up." Misty sighed. "I'm trying to do the work I need to do."

"The process can sometimes feel like a roller coaster of emotions until you become more confident in yourself. When you're frustrated, take a deep breath and speak calmly about your expectations. If you feel someone is putting you down, quietly state your position and face the issue. Pretty soon, you'll find you have no problem speaking for yourself, even if those around you don't agree with what you're saying. That's fine. We're all entitled to our own thoughts and opinions."

"I'm practicing a variety of ways to respond to situations that make me uncomfortable. And I'm building my sense of trust in others."

"All good things," said Susie. "I'm proud of you. Your confidence will grow as you continue standing up for yourself and responding to others in various ways. It's sort of like planting a seedling and watching it take root."

"Thanks," said Misty. She paused and then threw her arms around Susie.

CHAPTER THIRTEEN

MISTY HUNG THE CLOTHES SHE'D BEEN GIVEN IN HER closet at home or stowed them in her dresser drawers. She was trying to decide what to do for dinner when someone rang the doorbell.

Misty opened the door and found Hazel standing there. "You're back!"

Hazel smiled at her and stared at Sugar, who'd dutifully barked and was already wiggling in anticipation of expected attention.

"You got a dog!" said Hazel. "She's adorable!" She bent to stroke Sugar and murmured sweetly to her. "How did this happen?" she asked Misty.

"It's a long story. Come in, and I'll tell you. Do you have time for a glass of wine? I was trying to decide what to have for dinner, but your return calls for a celebration at Jake's."

"A glass of wine would be great. Dinner at Jake's, too."

Hazel followed her into the kitchen and took a seat at the table. "So, what's going on?" she asked.

"Let me pour the wine, and then I'll give you all the awful details."

Misty opened the bottle of wine, poured each of them a

glass, and then took a seat at the table opposite Hazel. She told about JoEllen seeing a man named Vince and fleshed out the story from there.

"Oh, my God! No wonder you freaked out when you thought it was Vince Tucci. I've heard enough about him to be scared for you. And David Graham is a sweetheart. He has a big crush on you, you know."

"David's a sweet guy, and I'm very interested in him. But I can't move forward until I feel more secure about myself and safe. He's going to teach me some karate moves. I've promised to attend a class before I go to Jake's. Want to come with me?"

"Sure, I'll join you. It should be fun."

"How was your trip home?" Misty asked her.

Hazel sighed and shook her head. "Let's just say it's best that I live far enough away from my parents that they aren't dropping in on me very often. They always thought I'd marry the son of their friends and live a life like theirs in the same town. I told them I just couldn't and wouldn't do it, that I was beginning a whole new life here in New Hampshire for a very positive reason."

"And?"

"And they don't understand. They think I'm selfish and mean for doing so," said Hazel, looking unhappy.

"Well, it's too late now. You've been hired to teach, and we want you here in Lilac Lake."

"Thanks. I needed to hear that." Hazel slung an arm around Misty's shoulder. "Karate, huh?"

#

That evening, Misty and Hazel drove to a one-story red-brick building outside of town where Kung Fu Karate held their classes. David drove up in his truck and parked beside them.

He waved and stepped out of the truck wearing a typical white karate uniform with a black belt tied at his waist. His feet were in flip-flops.

Misty noticed a small bit of chest hair where the V-neckline of the wrap top exposed it and remembered seeing him in his swimming trunks. No doubt about it, David was a sexy, ripped guy.

"Glad to see to see you here," David said. "You, too, Hazel."

Hazel looked pleased. "Misty invited me along, and I was excited about the invitation. It's smart for women to learn to defend themselves."

"What you will see here tonight is more formal than what I'll teach you, but I wanted you to see the real deal. It's much more than performing physical moves."

He led them inside where several teenagers were waiting. Instead of that age group's usual restlessness and hijinks, the kids stood quietly, waiting for their class to begin.

David greeted them with a little bow. "Good evening, class."

The students bowed. "Good evening, Sensei."

"Tonight, we have two special guests who will be observing. I thought I'd quickly review the elements of karate with you so that our guests understand what each of you might be doing."

The teens lined up.

"How many elements of karate are there?" David asked them.

"Four," said a girl, stepping forward. "Basic, Form, Study, and Sparring." She bowed and stepped back in line.

"Correct," said David. "Kihon is basic techniques, Kata is form or pattern, Bunkai is the study of techniques in Kata, and Kumite is free sparring. Tonight, we will be working on Kihon and Kata." He turned to Misty and Hazel. "Please have a seat and make yourselves comfortable watching. Karate basics include blocks, strikes, kicks, and different stances."

Misty watched from her seat in a chair against the wall as the students moved their bodies, arms, and hands in similar poses together.

"It doesn't look that dangerous," whispered Hazel.

As if he'd heard, David said, "It's essential to strengthen your body to do this Kata efficiently and well. When you put them together, it provides a great means of self-defense."

Mesmerized, Misty watched David teach his class, admiring the control he had over his body. She realized the strength and discipline some of the moves took, especially when combining them.

"How is this going to help us?" Hazel asked Misty softly.

"I'm not sure. But David will show us," Misty said.

After the class was over, David and the students placed their hands together and bowed. After a moment of silence,

David said, "Namaste."

The students broke into groups, and Misty and Hazel stood.

David came over to them. "What did you think?"

"It's interesting to watch, but how will that help Hazel and me protect ourselves?" asked Misty.

David gave her a knowing look. "I'm going to show you a few moves that incorporate some, not all, of this."

"Thanks. We'll meet you at Jake's. Okay?"

"Sounds good. I've got a change of clothes with me. I'll see you there."

As Misty and Hazel climbed into Misty's car, Hazel let out a long sigh. "Talk about sexy. And yet he's such a sweet guy. I swear if I didn't think he was interested in you, I'd go after him for myself."

Hearing Hazel talk about David that way, Misty felt a flash of jealousy. "I still have some things from my past to take care of before I'll be ready for a deeper relationship with him." Misty didn't say the thought of being intimate with a man, being that vulnerable with him, scared her to death.

"I'm sorry. I understand," said Hazel, giving her a sympathetic look. "Let's have some fun at Jake's. I'm ready for it."

When they walked into Jake's, Misty's spirits lifted. It was always satisfying to see these people who meant so much to her. Since coming back home, she felt as if this town was where she was supposed to be. She understood better that she was judged as the person she'd become, not the child of an addict.

Misty was amused when she saw Hazel's eyes light up as she was introduced to Gage. Poppy came into Jake's at the same time as David, and Misty and the others quickly made room for them at the table.

Crystal walked in with Emmett, and after being seated, she said casually. "I don't know what anyone has planned for Labor Day this year, but Emmett and I are hosting a picnic on the Saturday before the Monday holiday for those who want to come."

"That will be fantastic," said Taylor. "What should I bring?"

"Just bring yourselves. I'll have some food available, and I want to keep it simple. But thanks," said Crystal.

Misty couldn't look at her sister for fear of giving away the secret wedding. But she saw that beneath the blasé attitude Crystal was putting on, she was excited.

"Don't you and Hazel start school tomorrow?" Crystal asked her, deftly changing the subject.

"Tomorrow, we have a teacher's meeting for staff. We have a few days of meetings and time in our classrooms, and then school begins for the students for three days before the holiday," said Misty.

"You're both teachers?" Gage asked.

The conversation turned to upcoming schedules for

everyone, and Misty recognized that her favorite summer season was ending, and life would change at least a little for most of them.

Melissa and Ross arrived.

"Sorry we're late," said Melissa, "but I've been talking to Nettie at the café, and I think Crystal and I can hold our first gourmet dinner there in early October."

"Why so late?" asked Dani.

"It takes time to plan and organize," said Melissa, looking flustered as she glanced at Crystal.

"We want it done right," said Crystal, smiling at Melissa.

That's when Misty realized that Melissa must be helping with food for the wedding. To change the topic, she said, "Hazel and I are taking karate self-defense lessons from David."

"Oh," said JoEllen, "I want them too."

David shook his head. "Let me see how the private lessons go before I try to set up a class."

"I'd be interested in having you do a class for my police officers," said Nick.

"Okay. I was just trying to make Misty feel safer, but I'll see about working on a class for others."

"Any word on Misty's ex?" Dani asked Nick.

Nick shook his head and turned to JoEllen. "You haven't seen or talked to the man since you saw him?"

"No," said JoEllen. "Why would you ask?"

Nick shrugged. "Just checking."

"I didn't know it would cause such a flap. I should've kept my mouth closed," grumped JoEllen.

"No," said Nick. "We all need to keep an eye out for any stranger. In Misty's case, her ex is someone who could hurt her."

A shiver, like a spider's legs, crept across Misty's shoulders. She straightened, brushing aside the feeling. She had to be strong and move ahead with her life. Her body had healed. Now, it was time for the rest of her to become healthy again.

After the gang began breaking up, David said, "I've arranged to use the building for your first lesson tomorrow at the same time as today. Can you make it?"

"Yes," said Misty. "I have teacher's training tomorrow, but that's not scheduled for all day. I'll let Hazel know."

He tipped his head. "Okay, see you then."

As they studied each other, Misty liked David's attention and felt a pull of attraction to him. When she was stronger emotionally, she wanted to see where a relationship with him could go. Until then, she hoped he understood.

Misty walked to her front door, and as she took her time to unlock it, she heard Sugar barking on the other side.

When she opened the door, Sugar wiggled her tail so hard she fell on the floor.

Laughing, Misty bent down to help her and was rewarded with yips of welcome and kisses on the cheek.

"Okay, let's see how you did," said Misty, walking inside.

In the kitchen, where Sugar's bed had been tucked into a corner, the bed now sat in a patch of light by the sliding door.

"Clever dog," said Misty, opening the sliding door to let Sugar outside.

Misty watched the dog run across the lawn and then through the woods and sighed with gratitude. Sugar was a nice addition.

Her cell phone rang.

She checked the unknown Florida number, and a feeling of dread overcame her. At the thought it might be Vince, nausea rolled over her in a giant wave. Misty gripped the counter and held on. When she could lift her head, she drew a deep breath to calm herself. She'd blocked Vince's number and those of his friends and changed her cell phone number. But in today's world of computerized information, anyone had an excellent chance of being found.

The phone stopped ringing and then began again.

Hands trembling, she checked caller ID. *Crystal.*

"H-h-hello," she answered, unable to control her shaking voice.

"Hi, Misty. What's wrong?" asked Crystal.

"I just had an earlier phone call. I didn't recognize the number, but it came from Florida, and I thought it might be Vince."

"Oh, Misty. I don't like the sound of that. What can I do to help?"

"I've got a dog, I'm taking self-defense lessons, I have pepper spray and a whistle. I don't know what else I can do."

"I have an idea. I'll talk to you later." Crystal hung up.

Misty plopped down in a kitchen chair and rubbed Sugar's ears. Still unable to shake her bad feelings, Misty went to check the rest of the rooms inside the house.

A short while later, the doorbell rang.

She went to answer it and was surprised to see a workman there.

"You Misty Owen?" he asked.

"Yes, what can I help you with?" she asked, holding onto Sugar's collar. Her friendly dog was growling.

He indicated the red truck behind him. "Sorry it's so late. I was making another call in town and was asked to stop by. I'm Jim from AAA Security. I'm here to discuss a security system."

"But I didn't request one," she said.

"No, but Dr. Emmett Chambers did," explained the man. "May I come in and take a look around?" He handed her the order.

Misty checked the truck and the badge on the man's work shirt and called Crystal.

"It's true. We did order it for you," said Crystal.

"Thanks," said Misty. "I had to be sure."

"As you should," Crystal said. "Talk to you later."

Knowing everything was okay, Misty allowed the workman to come inside and followed him as he went from room to room, making notes on a notepad he carried with him.

When he was through, he said, "It's a pretty simple set up. I'll return tomorrow with everything I need, and we'll get the job done."

"I won't be here, but I'll find someone to let you in," said Misty. "Probably my sister, Crystal Owen."

The man bobbed his head. "That's who called me."

As soon as he left in his truck, Misty called her sister. "Thanks, Crystal, for arranging for me to have a security system. That's such a generous gift."

"Thank Emmett. He's the one who insisted we do it," said Crystal. "We'll both feel better knowing it's installed. And I've already set aside time to be at your house while the work is being done."

Misty let out a sigh of gratitude. Her sister was once again taking care of her. And now, Emmett, too.

CHAPTER FOURTEEN

MISTY GOT DRESSED IN A PAIR OF SLACKS SUSIE HAD given her and a flowing green top. After learning how important it was, she wore comfy sandals on her feet.

Her shoulder-length dark hair hung straight instead of in the ponytail she preferred on a hot summer day.

Today was the first day of the school year, and she'd meet with her colleagues for the first time before students arrived later in the week. She was a bit nervous. She looked younger than twenty-six, which was no problem with the kids, but sometimes older teachers had to be shown how effective she was as a teacher before they accepted her.

Sugar stared up at her and wagged her tail.

Misty hugged her. "You must be a good girl today. I'll be back as soon as I can."

She'd taken Sugar for an early morning walk, but being home alone for a day was a test for both of them.

At the sound of the doorbell, Misty went to answer it.

Hazel greeted her. "Hi! Are you ready?"

"Yes," said Misty, feeling her excitement grow. She grabbed her purse, said goodbye to Sugar, and locked the front door.

"Before we get in the car for our training, I want to take a selfie with you," said Hazel.

Misty put an arm around Hazel and smiled at Hazel's request. She loved having such a close friend. They'd instantly clicked.

"David will meet us later today at the Kung Fu Karate Studio," said Misty as she climbed into Hazel's light-blue VW convertible.

"I'm relieved it's just going to be the two of us for now," said Hazel. "I'm not that athletic."

"Bet you were a cute cheerleader, though," said Misty.

Hazel laughed. "I practiced a lot."

A few minutes later, they arrived at the school, which was on the outer edge of the center of town. The day was going to be one of learning names and new procedures.

Her former third-grade teacher approached her.

"Hi, Mrs. Walters," Misty said, beaming at her.

"Misty Owens!" She took hold of both of Misty's hands and squeezed. "I was delighted to learn you were teaching here at Emerson Wittner Elementary. It's always satisfying to know that one of my special former students has chosen to be a teacher. I'm here to help you in any way I can. And please call me Marilyn."

Warmth flooded through her. Misty remembered how Mrs. Walters had made her feel special. Misty couldn't stop herself from giving her a quick hug. "You're the reason I've always loved the idea of teaching. You were the best teacher I ever had. You made a difference in my life."

"Ah, thank you. It was my privilege to have you as a student, and now it's a privilege to work with you. Come to me anytime. I'm here if you need me." Mrs. Walters left her to join other teachers.

Misty was thrilled to learn she'd have only nineteen students in her class. In Florida, she'd had twenty-eight. This would allow her to provide more one-on-one time with both high-achieving students and those who struggled.

Hazel had been assigned to third-grade students and was in a classroom next to hers, which made Misty feel relieved. If necessary, they could spell one another for emergency bathroom breaks.

After the morning meeting, Misty went to check her classroom. During the summer, she'd bought supplies and books, and she and Hazel had set up her classroom, placing tables the way she wanted them. She gave it a critical look and decided to make a few changes.

Her theme for her classroom was kindness, so she posted the "Kindness" banner she'd made so it would greet the kids when they entered the room. She could hardly wait to see their faces when they saw the colorful posters she'd hung and the bookshelves she'd filled. She loved the idea of rewarding kids for good behavior with reading time.

###

A lunch of pizza and salad was a catered affair in the cafeteria. Misty was reminded of how kids formed certain groups and watched as the adults seemed to do the same, sitting at tables of four.

The principal, Nolan Deere, remained standing alone on the sidelines as if he wanted to remind everyone that he was in charge. He'd recently been transferred from the high school and was still an "unknown" as a leader of the elementary school. Misty privately thought he was a gruff man but was awaiting judgment on how well he performed his role.

Marilyn Walter waved Misty and Hazel over to her table, and another second-grade teacher sat with them.

After lunch, the group headed into the gym for another training session, and then Misty and Hazel were free to leave.

Misty couldn't wait to check on Sugar.

Misty arrived home to find a note attached to her front door. She opened it and read instructions from Crystal on how to operate her new security system. She could hear Sugar barking and hurried to unlock the front door and go to the control panel mounted by the front door, as Crystal had indicated. She punched in the security code, and the light on the panel turned green.

She hugged Sugar, let her outside, and then went through the house, reviewing Crystal's message about how the system had been set up. She checked the windows where sensors had been installed. Misty didn't think it would be necessary to have the system on when she was at home during the day. But it would be a big relief at night.

Crystal called to see how her day had gone and to check on how the security system was working.

After Misty filled her in on both, Crystal said, "Emmett's mother is arriving a few days before the wedding. His father is coming on Saturday morning and will leave on Sunday. Of course, he's making a political trip out of it, but we don't care. It's much easier on Emmett's mother when his father isn't around."

"Sad, but I get it. I'm relieved you and his mother are getting along," said Misty.

"Me, too," said Crystal. "Natalie Chamberlain is a much different woman now that she's sober."

"Do you want me to plan a luncheon for you and Natalie? Or anyone else you want to invite?"

"It's sweet of you to offer," said Crystal, "but Nettie has already invited us to the Café, and I'm anxious for Natalie to see it so she can understand what Melissa and I are planning to do there."

"There must be something I can do as Maid of Honor," said Misty.

"Just having you there with me is all I need. As soon as people start to arrive, we'll disappear into the house to change. Whitney will help gather the people into a circle. Nick and Emmett will leave the house first, then us. We'll appear from the back of the house and walk into the middle of the group for the ceremony. We have a guitar player and a justice of the peace lined up."

"So, everyone will be standing?" Misty asked.

"That's the only way we could manage it," said Crystal, "though we'll have a chair available for GG and any others that might need it. We thought about having a sit-down dinner, but then it quickly became something neither Emmett nor I wanted. But we will have a tent for the buffet in case of inclement weather. We envision this as a loving ceremony with friends we care about."

"What about the food? Last night, I guessed Melissa was helping with that," said Misty.

"Melissa, Nettie, and Jason are preparing the food, which I know will be delicious. We'll have a keg of beer, wine, and soft drinks available along, with the usual cold water."

"What about the honeymoon?" asked Mindy, excited for her sister.

"That's a surprise. All Emmett has told me was to pack lightly and bring an appetite." Crystal's voice rose with excitement. "We leave the morning after the ceremony."

"It all sounds wonderful," gushed Misty. "When you return, I'll do something special for you."

"Thanks. I know these plans are a little unorthodox, but Emmett and I are excited about them."

"That's all that matters. Should we get our nails done on Saturday morning? My treat?"

"Yes, that would be fun. I thought about having my hair done and decided to leave it as it is. That's how Emmett likes it."

"Okay, I'll make an appointment at the Nail Parlor," Misty said, relieved to be able to do something for Crystal.

Crystal said goodbye, and Misty ended the call. Life was moving fast. She hoped she was ready for all of it.

Misty picked up Hazel, and they headed to their karate lesson. After seeing the traditional uniform on David's students, Misty and Hazel were both wearing tights and a T-shirt.

David met them in shorts and a T-shirt. "Great to see you." He led them inside the building to a small classroom and took off his shoes. "This is informal training, so we don't need uniforms, but we'll be working on some of the traditional movements before we get into more of a self-defense mode. By doing it this way, I hope you'll be more aware of your bodies and how to use quick movements to your advantage."

Misty nodded solemnly. She had told only Crystal about the phone call from Florida and decided not to mention it to anyone else. She slipped off her sandals and stood ready.

David demonstrated a move and then asked Hazel and her to mimic it.

After completing several repetitive moves, Misty felt more in control of her body. She wasn't ready to confront anyone yet, but she could understand the value of the exercise.

Another instructor arrived, and he and David demonstrated some sparring moves.

"See how you can use your movements to protect yourself," said David. He suddenly kicked out one leg and his sparring partner whirled away and then fell when David followed up with a strike of his hand to his neck.

"I don't want you to do that to me," Hazel whispered to Misty.

Misty laughed. "I have only one person in mind when I'm practicing this."

By the end of their class, Misty had a better appreciation for the skills involved and realized how skilled David was.

"Anyone going to Jake's?" Hazel asked.

"I'm not. But I'd be happy to give you a ride," said Misty.

"Okay, if I stop by and see you, Misty?" asked David. "I'd like to talk to you about something."

"Sure," she said. "That would be nice." He looked like he wanted to do more than talk, and she liked the idea.

After dropping Hazel off at Jake's, Misty drove home excited to have some time alone with David. They'd both been busy, and she'd missed being with him. She thought about him all the time. David was a great guy, and she didn't want to lose the growing relationship she had with him.

He pulled his truck in behind her car.

While she waited for him to join her at the front door, she worked on the security system and rushed inside to turn it off.

David stood at the front entrance laughing while Sugar raced in circles, running to Misty and then over to him.

Misty picked her up and then handed her to David. "We're both excited to see you."

His eyes focused on her, and a bright smile lit them. "I'm glad. We haven't had many chances to be together."

"No," she agreed. "Come in. How about something cold to drink? Beer? Lemonade? Iced Tea?

"Ice water is fine for me after that workout," said David.

"You're really good, you know," said Misty, handing him a glass of water. "We can sit outside where it's cool."

"Okay. It's a nice night."

Sugar followed him out to the deck while Misty grabbed a glass of water for herself.

David had placed his glass on the table and stood at the deck railing looking into the woods. A moon hovered above them shedding silvery light on the trees around them.

"It's almost magical, isn't it?" murmured Misty, standing beside him, gazing into their surroundings. The sound of the river's flowing water was like music on a night like this.

David turned to her and gave her a questioning look. "May I?"

Misty's pulse pounded. She lifted her face to his, and when his lips met hers, she shivered with delight. Being with David was so different from what she'd known. He cupped her cheeks with his hands and moved closer.

Though she could feel his arousal, she wasn't scared. And as his kiss deepened, she welcomed it.

When they finally pulled apart, David studied her with such a tender expression she wanted to weep. She laid her head on his shoulder and held on tight.

"On the nights we can't be together, let's talk on the phone, keep things going," said David.

"That would be great. I want to move forward with you," said Misty, grateful for the work she'd put in to enable her to speak openly with him.

"Me too," murmured David, leaning down to kiss her, stopping the conversation, and letting his lips speak to her in a heart-stopping way.

Long after David left, Misty replayed the evening in her mind.

CHAPTER FIFTEEN

THE MORNING OF THE FIRST SCHOOL DAY WITH HER students, Misty checked her canvas bag once more to be sure she had everything she wanted. She liked to keep aspirin, Tums, breath mints, and a few other personal items in her desk. Her favorite water bottle was filled with ice water and tucked inside the bag. Star "Welcome" stickers for each student were ready, along with a new book she intended to read to them in the afternoon when she knew they'd be tired and a bit restless.

Hazel beeped her car horn, and Misty said goodbye to Sugar. Then, she activated the alarm system and closed and locked the front door.

"Ready?" asked Hazel when Misty climbed into the car. "I can't wait to meet my kids."

Misty smiled. "I'm taking a photo of each child and mounting them on one of the bulletin boards. The last class I taught loved that."

"We missed you at Jake's last night, but nothing exciting was going on. I didn't stay long. Everyone is talking about going to Crystal and Emmett's picnic over the weekend, but nothing super big is happening in town. Just the usual holiday sales and neighborhood picnics."

"Labor Day celebrations are pretty tame compared to 4th of July," said Misty. "It's a time to change gears from summer to fall."

"Dani invited me to use the lake facilities at The Meadows. Are you interested in taking their canoe out on the lake with me?"

"That would be fun. It's always beautiful there."

They pulled into the school's parking lot.

Anxious to get inside, Misty grabbed her things from the backseat of the car and waited for Hazel to walk inside with her.

They took another selfie of them together and began their first day with the kids.

In her classroom, Misty posted the names of each of her students alphabetically on the bulletin board leaving spaces for photographs. It was a way for her to learn the names and faces of her students and was something the kids loved, almost like seeing their photo on a refrigerator at home. In Florida, she'd loved comparing the first day of school photos to the last day of school. There was always such obvious growth.

The students started arriving.

Wearing a large name tag, Misty greeted each child and handed them a "Welcome" sticker to put on the back of their hands.

As soon as all her students had arrived, received a warm

welcome, and were seated at one of the round tables, Misty closed the door, introduced herself, and talked about her expectations of them being like a family, with everyone getting along and showing kindness to everyone.

As they created artistic designs on their name tags, she took a photo of each child and asked a simple question about him or her. She loved the children's openness at this age. Living in a small town, the children represented different parts of it, from a fireman's daughter to the son of a worker at Beckman's Lumber.

Misty did her best to connect with each of them, but afterward, her thoughts kept returning to the little boy whose father worked at Collister Construction. Brody Kirk hadn't smiled yet, would only whisper, and looked scared. Misty knew that kind of behavior. She'd lived it.

Later, Misty checked to see which parents would show up at school to pick up their child and which child was assigned to a bus. Brody was assigned to a bus. She was disappointed not to meet a parent of his but decided she'd keep a close eye on him. She'd felt a special connection to the boy who reminded her so much of herself at that age.

When it was time, she walked her class to the front of the school, where parents and the school buses were waiting. The bus lines were well-organized, and Misty watched over her children, making sure all were picked up.

The principal was standing outside.

Misty went to speak to him. "Hi, Nolan. I have a student

I'm concerned about. I think there may be something going on at home."

A tall man, he looked down at her. "Ms. Owen, this is the first day of school. Certainly, you aren't so judgmental that you would assign trouble where there isn't any."

"I'm just looking for guidance here," Misty spoke calmly, though her heart was racing.

He moved away, and Misty stared at his retreating figure with dismay. *How dare he disregard her concerns without even asking any questions?*

Marilyn Walters came over to her. "I couldn't help overhearing your conversation. I'm sorry. Nolan Deere is just protecting himself. Date and document everything when dealing with him. Include me as someone who was present and can confirm your conversation. He may be new here at the school, but his reputation of being non-supportive to teachers precedes him."

"Thanks," said Misty. "I don't mean to judge harshly, but I think there's a real issue."

"Just be careful," said Marilyn.

Frustrated, Misty went back to straighten her classroom.

On the way home, Misty told Hazel about her conversation with the principal.

"I'd heard he was difficult, but regardless, he knows if we suspect physical abuse, we're required by law to report it. You didn't see any bruises on the boy, did you?"

Misty shook her head. "I'll keep watch for it, though."

"How were the other kids?" Hazel asked.

"Adorable. How about yours?" Misty asked her.

"A good group, but large," said Hazel. "I'm glad I have a TA. There are a couple of troublemakers, but my TA and I have already told them that's not allowed in our class."

"It's nice you have a TA. But with my class, I'll be fine," said Misty.

"I'll need all the help I can get. For some reason, the third-grade classes are much larger than some others," said Hazel. "I'm too tired to go to Jake's, but there are a couple of guys I want to get to know better."

"Want to talk about it?" asked Misty, giving her a teasing smile.

"Not yet," said Hazel, laughing.

Misty came home, exhausted. Thinking she'd rest for a moment, she sat on the couch, mentally reviewing everything she needed to do the next day. She was startled awake sometime later when the chime of her cell tugged her awake. *Crystal.*

"I know it's the first day of school, but why don't you come over to say hello to Emmett's mother?"

Misty knew from the anxious tone in Crystal's voice that she wanted help. Natalie Chamberlain had been a first-class snob before she'd sobered up, but even now, Crystal was still a little intimidated by her.

Sighing with regret, Misty said, "I wish I could, but I'm afraid I'll fall back to sleep on the way over. I'm exhausted. The first few days of school are physically and mentally grueling. I'll come over tomorrow after I have a power nap. I promise."

"Okay, I'll see you tomorrow. Talk to you later," said Crystal.

Misty ended the call, grateful for Crystal's understanding. Many people had no idea teaching was a difficult job.

The next morning, Misty awaited the children in her classroom, excited to show them the pictures she'd posted of them on the bulletin board. She also planned to ask students' parents to volunteer for one-on-one reading sessions. She wouldn't go to the principal until she had a few parents interested.

Her students arrived en masse. There were a few tears from two children that quickly went away after they sat in their chairs at their tables, where Misty had placed a worksheet in front of each one.

"First of all, I thought you might want to see what our class looks like in pictures. Each one of you is a member of this class. Remember, our class motto is 'KINDNESS.' That means we are kind and helpful and nice to each other."

Her students, even Brody, agreed as one.

"Good. Now, on three, what is our motto? One, two, three."

"Kindness" came a chorus of replies.

"We're going to remember that every day," said Misty, directing them to go to the paper on their tables.

While her students worked, Misty walked around the room to assess each child's skills. She quickly picked out a few who might need extra help. Though he hadn't interacted with the others earlier, Brody wasn't one of them.

Later, when the children lined up to go outside to play at recess, Brody hung back.

"It's time to go outside for some fresh air. I think you'll enjoy it." She studied him. "Don't worry. You'll be fine there. I'll see to it."

Misty led him outside and watched as he sat on the ground under a tree and studied the kids running on the playground. A sweet girl in her class, Violet Allen, went over and sat beside him. They didn't talk, but neither did Brody move away.

When the bell rang for the students to line up, Violet took Brody's hand, and they came to the line together. Observing them, tears blurred Misty's vision. It reminded her how lucky she'd been to have found friends in school.

After school, Misty came home, set her alarm for thirty minutes, and collapsed on her bed with Sugar by her side. After her nap, she'd visit Crystal and Natalie. She couldn't let

Crystal down. Her sister didn't ask too much of her, and Misty knew that any break with Natalie would be appreciated.

When her alarm sounded, Misty got up, feeling somewhat rested.

Wiggling with happiness, Sugar waited for Misty to freshen up, and then they both climbed into Misty's car.

As Misty entered the driveway of Emmett's house, she took a moment to study her surroundings. Since purchasing the house from Dr. Johnson, who formerly had lived here, Emmett had made a lot of changes to the house. Collister Construction had helped to update both the interior and exterior, and with a fresh coat of light-gray paint, the building sparkled. Graham Landscaping had updated the landscaping, adding new plants, flowers, and a few touches like stone or wood benches. Seeing it now, as she headed out back, Misty thought the setting was superb for a wedding.

Sugar ran ahead. Laughing, Misty tried to keep up with her. She approached the screened-in porch out of breath and saw Crystal sitting there with Natalie.

"Hello," said Misty, climbing the few steps.

Crystal opened the door. "Welcome. Natalie and I were just sitting here admiring the view."

"It's a lovely sight, isn't it?" said Misty, holding out her hand to Natalie.

"You remember my sister, Misty," Crystal said to her.

"Yes, it's nice to see you," said Natalie, smiling and shaking her hand.

"I'm glad you could come to town a little early," said Misty. "I'd like you to join Crystal and me at our favorite nail salon on Saturday morning. My treat."

"That's very kind of you," said Natalie. "I just had my nails done while I was staying at our summer place in Maine, but I'm sure they could do with some refreshing."

"You must be excited about the wedding," said Misty, and she watched as Natalie struggled to smile. "I was hoping it could take place in Maine, but I understand the problems it might present by doing so."

"Many of Natalie's old friends are in Maine. But it would mean making the wedding larger than we wanted. That, and the conflict with Emmett's father," explained Crystal.

At this, Natalie's lips narrowed, but she said nothing.

Misty knew a major reason Crystal and Emmett wanted a small wedding in Lilac Lake was dealing with his parents. Small and simple is what Crystal and Emmett told everyone they wanted—a joyous occasion. With Natalie and Everett Chamberlain together, that was almost impossible. Though they presented an impression to the press of being happily married, everyone knew it was just to win votes for Everett.

"Well, I think having the wedding here is going to be beautiful. Emmett has become a well-respected member of the town. We all love how he treats everyone—adults and children—as his patients."

"I'm not surprised. Emmett has always been interested in helping others. And I know he's grown to love this town,"

Natalie admitted.

"Has Natalie met GG?" Misty asked.

Crystal smiled at them. "We're having lunch tomorrow. I know they'll like meeting one another." She explained to Natalie, "GG is the grandmother many of us think of as our own. She's a very generous woman who's made a great impact in our small town."

"She seems lovely," said Natalie. Her face lit up when Emmett walked into the room.

"Great to see you women chatting," he said, giving Crystal a kiss on the cheek before greeting his mother the same way. "Let me change my clothes, and then we'll head to the Lilac Lake Inn for dinner. Are you coming too, Misty?"

Misty shook her head. "Thanks, but I have to prepare for school tomorrow."

"How's it going?" Emmett asked. "You start up again after Labor Day?"

"Yes," she said. "It's been going well. The kids are very cute at that age." She wouldn't say anything about her concerns for Brody but knew if the time came when she should, Emmett would be a great help. "I want to thank both of you for the security system you had installed at my house. It was such a nice thing to do."

"We thought it was important," said Emmett. "Both of us feel better about you having it. The same security service is doing one for our house, too."

"They seemed to do an excellent job," said Crystal. "I

assume you got all my notes on it."

Misty chuckled. "It'll take me a while to get used to it, but I think you covered everything."

Sugar barked at the door, and Crystal let Sugar inside.

"Oh, my! What a cute dog," said Natalie.

Sugar went right over to her and sat by her feet, allowing Natalie to stroke her head.

"She's trained as a therapy dog," said Misty, watching Sugar do her thing as if the dog knew instinctively that Natalie needed attention.

"Maybe we should get you a dog, Natalie," said Crystal.

Natalie shook her head firmly. "I'll be traveling for Everett and can't handle a dog. But maybe later. This one is darling."

Misty and Crystal exchanged looks of surprise, and then Misty stood. "I'd better be going, but I'm pleased to see you, Natalie."

"Thank you," said Natalie, studying her.

Misty forced a smile and pushed away thoughts of not measuring up, even though that's exactly how Natalie made her feel.

Crystal, ever the big sister, walked over and gave her a hug. "Thanks for stopping by, sis."

Happy she'd made the effort to come, Misty left with Sugar, knowing the weekend ahead wouldn't be easy.

Friday night, following a one-hour nap, Misty sat in Jake's.

She needed to be with friends for their usual end-of-week celebrations. Even those with children, like Whitney and Beth Beckham, got babysitters so they could join in. And tonight was special because Crystal and Emmett's surprise wedding would take place tomorrow.

Misty noticed that Melissa and Ross hadn't joined them and suspected Melissa was busy prepping some of the food for the wedding.

Conversation, as usual, was easy among the group. Everyone was eager to celebrate the long weekend.

"A picnic at Crystal and Emmett's place is a great way to start the holiday," said Dirk. "Any idea what to take to it?" he asked her.

Misty worked hard not to give anything away. "My understanding is no one needs to bring anything. Crystal and Melissa are practicing catering, and everything will be prepared in time for the picnic at four o'clock."

"If you come to Lilac Lake Cottage on Monday, you need to bring your own drinks and a dish to pass," said Dani. "You can come when you want and leave when you're ready." She faced the group. "That goes for everyone. Right, Whitney? Taylor?"

At their nods, the conversation returned to the Gilford girls' annual party.

Misty used that opportunity to slip away from the crowd. She had to see her sister and make sure everything was on track for the wedding.

###

When she arrived at Emmett's house, all was quiet. Too quiet. Misty sat in her car, wondering what was wrong. She called her sister, and Crystal answered right away.

"What's going on?" Misty asked. "It sounds as if you've been crying."

"It's Emmett's father. He's such a bastard," said Crystal. "He arrived this afternoon ahead of time to talk to us. He's arranged for a journalist to do an article on him, and he's hired a photographer to take pictures at our wedding. This whole thing is all BS. Emmett can barely stand his stepfather. He's gone to the Inn to talk to him again, trying to explain that this is our wedding, not another opportunity for his campaign."

"Okay, I'm coming inside," said Misty. She wanted to hug her sister and find a way to help her.

"Please do," Crystal said. "I need to calm down, and talking to you will help."

Misty found Crystal lying down in the master bedroom.

She sat up when she saw Misty. "Thanks for coming. I didn't want anyone to know what was happening. This is supposed to be a happy occasion. It's just like Emmett's stepfather to do something like this."

"We'll just have to work around him," said Misty. "Let's call a security company to keep uninvited people away, including any journalist or photographer Everett has hired. We won't make a fuss about it; just quietly take care of it."

Crystal hugged her. "That's exactly what we'll do. I'm sure

Emmett won't mind. This way, there won't be any confrontation with his stepfather. It'll be a done deal."

Together, sitting on the bed, they looked up information online and found a company in Portsmouth that provided security guards. Crystal called and left a message. Moments later, she received a return call. After arranging for someone to come tomorrow afternoon, Crystal ended the call and turned to Misty. "Thank you for thinking of this. It'll make me feel better, and neither Emmett nor I will have to be involved in turning Everett's people away."

"How are things going with Emmett's mother?" Misty asked.

"Okay. Once she gets comfortable with me, she can be sweet. And not having a daughter, Natalie loves knowing the details of the wedding. Thank you for inviting her to have her nails done. She is grateful to be part of the wedding."

"How's Natalie doing with Emmett's stepfather?"

"It's something I don't understand," admitted Crystal. "She's willing to help him politically in the background, something she's done for years. I think she feels beholden to him for rescuing her from a bad situation when she was a young single mother with a baby."

"To each his own," said Misty. "Families can be complicated. I'm lucky to have had you all these years acting as mother, father, and big sister."

"And I've had GG and others to turn to," said Crystal with a thoughtful expression. "Emmett and I will have the wedding we want because we'll stick together. It's a test, in a way, of what our lives will be like going forward."

"I think you're right to trust him," said Misty. "Look what he's given up to come to Lilac Lake. He could've been just a spoiled rich son of a politician instead of the general practitioner of a small town who desperately needs him."

"Absolutely," said Crystal. She studied Misty. "Where'd you get that smart?"

Misty held up a hand. "I think I've proven I'm not smart. I've made a bad mistake, and I'm praying I won't have to pay for it over and over again."

"Vince hasn't shown himself yet," said Crystal.

"What about the call from Florida?" asked Misty.

"It's worrisome," admitted Crystal, "but we're on alert now. And, really, you can't prove it was Vince. Maybe it was a misplaced phone call, a telemarketer."

Sugar barked, and Emmett entered the room.

"How did it go with Everett?" asked Crystal, getting to her feet and going over to him.

Emmett shook his head. "The man has no scruples and an ego that won't quit. I told him that we stand firm on our idea of a private wedding and that I won't allow him to use us for publicity. He seemed subdued, but he didn't actually agree not to use the wedding for his promotional purposes in the future."

Crystal drew a deep breath and let it out. "Misty and I have come up with a plan. We've arranged to hire a security guard to keep away strangers, including newspeople and photographers. I trust Belinda Buckley from Captured Moments to do a good job photographing for us. I've met her. She's new in town and trying to grow her business."

"I hate to say it, but I don't trust Everett to respect what we want," said Emmett.

"How's your mother holding up? Crystal asked him.

"As usual, she's coping and trying not to make matters worse." Emmett sighed. "I thought once she got sober, she might leave him. But I understand it would be financially difficult for her to do so. Instead, she and Everett have a living arrangement that works for them both."

Emmett put his arm around Crystal. "We're never going to be like that. I promise."

"I believe you. It's insane," said Crystal, giving him a kiss on the cheek.

Misty stood. "It's time I left. Crystal, I'll see you tomorrow at ten at the nail salon with Natalie."

"Sure thing. Thanks." Crystal hugged her. "Thanks for your support this evening. It made a big difference for me."

"It's about time I could help you," Misty said. "C'mon, Sugar. Let's go home."

Sugar wagged her tail and followed Misty to her car.

Misty knew she'd need all the rest she could get because tomorrow wouldn't be as easy as they'd hoped.

CHAPTER SIXTEEN

THE NEXT MORNING, MISTY AWOKE TO GRAYNESS. SHE got out of bed and raced to the window. Looking out at the thick, dark clouds in the sky, she let out a soft groan. The weatherman had mentioned a disturbance pushing through the area but had said no rain. She hoped he was right.

She turned on the weather channel. Again, no rain was mentioned.

Picking up her cell, she called Crystal. "Happy Wedding Day! I've checked, and though the weather looks iffy, there's a promise of no rain."

"I'm hoping that's the case, but I'm not worried. People should be here soon to put up the tent. We didn't want to take the chance of the day being ruined."

"Are you going to be ready for a visit to the nail salon with Natalie?"

"We'll see. She isn't feeling well, but I'm pretty sure it's a case of nerves, which tends to happen when Everett puts too much pressure on her. I'm going to pick her up shortly and take her to the Café for breakfast."

"Should I meet you there?" asked Misty.

"Would you? That would make it easier," Crystal responded.

"Sure. Why don't I meet you at 9:30?"

"Perfect," said Crystal. "It will seem like a long day until guests finally arrive. Emmett will be working with his temporary replacement for the medical practice until noon or so."

"In the meantime, let's have some fun. After the mani-pedis, I'll bring my dress over to your house and help you fix your hair."

"That would be great," said Crystal. "Whitney is going to help me too. That'll give us time for a little party, just the three of us. Nick will be hanging around the backyard early. He wants to make sure the area is secure."

"He's a good man," said Misty. Crystal had been married to Nick briefly until they both figured out that as much as they liked each other, marriage wasn't workable for them. They've been close friends ever since.

Misty ended the call with Crystal, dressed for her morning walk, and left the house with Sugar. It was a little time-consuming to reset the security alarm, but she felt better doing it.

As usual, she ended up at the Graham's memorial park for Lily. Misty felt a special connection to David when she was there. He'd sent a video about self-defense for her to watch and would give her some private lessons after the holiday.

As she sat on a bench staring at the pink roses she loved, she felt a calmness wash over her. David's mother appeared and walked over to her. "It's sweet that you spend time here."

"It's a lovely place to sit and contemplate things," said Misty.

"I agree," said Susie. "How did your first days of school go?"

Misty watched Susie pet Sugar. "They went well. Kids at that age are so cute. I must confess, though, that I'm worried about one student who seems fragile. I'll keep my eye on him."

"Some need a little extra encouragement," said Susie.

Misty sat straighter as a thought came to her. "Would you be willing to volunteer to help kids in my class with reading? I'm trying to set up a volunteer program for my class, and you'd be ideal for it."

"How much time are you talking about?" Susie asked.

"Maybe one afternoon a week?" said Misty, becoming excited about it.

"Sure. I can do that. I've been looking for a way to get out of the house and away from the landscape business for a bit."

"That's right. You handle all the office work for the company," said Misty. "This would be the total opposite of that."

Susie grinned. "Wednesdays would be best for me."

"Okay. I'll make a note of it. Thanks, Susie, for your help. I'm hoping to get enough people willing to volunteer."

"Just let me know." Susie got up and checked the rest of the area, picking up any debris, and then made her way to her car parked at the curb.

Misty realized the connection to David she felt here

extended to his family—even Lily.

She rose and walked out of the park with Sugar, excited about the possibility of her volunteer program.

Later, Misty rushed into the Lilac Lake Café, late for her meeting with Crystal and Natalie. She'd taken time to shampoo and smooth her hair, which was a challenge on this humid summer day.

"There you are," said Crystal, calling to her from a patio table where she sat with Natalie.

Misty hurried over and greeted them both, then sat. "I'm ready for a cup of coffee and something sweet."

Nettie approached them. "Hey, Misty. How are you? Now that school has started, I've missed seeing you and Sugar on your early morning walks."

"Thanks. Weekends are mine, though, and you'll see me then." Misty looked around. "I love some of the changes you've made to the décor. I guess that's how you're getting ready for the gourmet dinners, huh?"

"Yes. We're hoping to add something unique to the social scene with those dinners," said Nettie, smiling.

The interior walls were now painted a bold, rich green, giving the restaurant a nice look for an evening setting. Booths had been removed, and new tile flooring made to look like wood had been added. Finally, new natural wood tables replaced the old red tables.

"All this in just a couple of days," said Misty.

"We had to move quickly so we could keep the Café open for this holiday weekend," said Nettie.

"You're coming to the picnic, aren't you?" asked Misty.

"Oh, yes," said Nettie, her eyes sparkling. "The Café is closing a little early. Neither Jason nor I want to miss our first Labor Day picnic."

Crystal turned to Natalie. "Gourmet dinners is a very exciting project for Melissa and me. You'll have to come visit for one of them."

"We'll see. It'll be a busy fall with Everett's campaign," said Natalie politely.

Misty and Crystal exchanged looks of surprise, but neither said anything.

"What can I get you?' Nettie asked Misty. "Any refills for the two of you?" she asked Crystal and Natalie.

Misty ordered coffee and a croissant, and with no refills requested, Nettie walked away.

Crystal smiled at Misty. "Your hair looks nice."

"Thanks. I'm going to fix yours later today."

Natalie looked from one to the other. "It's sweet that you sisters are close."

Misty gave Crystal a pat on the shoulder. "Crystal more or less raised me. She's going to make a wonderful mother."

"Oh, my! I hope you have children quickly," Natalie said to Crystal. "I'm told grandchildren are a real blessing."

Misty could see that Crystal was uncomfortable.

"Emmett and Crystal will be excellent parents," Misty said, giving her sister an encouraging smile.

"I hope you have more than one child," said Natalie. "As a boy, Emmett always wanted siblings."

"One step at a time," said Crystal, chuckling. "I'm hoping we can get through this day."

Natalie's usual serious expression softened. "I'm sorry about Everett and his demands. I've tried to talk to him about it, but as usual, he's bent on having his own way."

"This time, he may have met his match," said Crystal sweetly, but Misty knew how determined she was.

Natalie held up her hand. "You'll have no trouble from me."

Misty's food came, and she ate quickly so they could be on their way to their appointment.

At the nail salon, Misty was relieved to see Natalie enjoying herself. She'd even told the manicurist that Crystal was her new daughter, which touched them all.

As they left, Natalie requested to go back to the Inn to rest before getting ready for the wedding.

"Why don't I take you in my car so Crystal can go home? I'm sure she has a lot of things to take care of there," said Misty.

"That would be nice," said Crystal.

"Okay, I'll see you later," said Natalie, giving Crystal an unexpected kiss on the cheek. "Anything to help on your big day."

Misty and Natalie said goodbye to Crystal and climbed into Misty's used gray Honda.

"It's not fancy, but it's perfect for me," said Misty, dusting an imaginary speck of dust from the passenger's front seat. Proud of the car, she kept it spotlessly clean.

"This is fine," said Natalie. "I appreciate the ride." She slid into the seat and waited while Misty went around the car and got behind the wheel.

On the way to the Lilac Lake Inn, Misty debated and said, "I'm glad you're supporting Crystal and Emmett. They're a wonderful couple and are very much a part of this community. I'm sorry that Emmett's stepfather is difficult."

"He's an important man," said Natalie, "but that doesn't make it right that he wants to overrule others' choices."

"I know he didn't support your sobriety at first. Crystal has told me how proud she is of you. Our mother wasn't as strong."

"I'm sorry," said Natalie. "It's a struggle, but I'm proud of myself too. That kind of attitude helps and is something I've had to learn to accept. All women should take a moment, recognize their own strengths, and applaud themselves as they move forward."

"Yes," said Misty, aware of the times she didn't feel strong.

"Simply surviving is a sign of strength," Natalie said, and Misty wondered if that's how Natalie made her marriage work.

CHAPTER SEVENTEEN

Misty went to Emmett's house and into the backyard. Though it had been a gray morning, the sky had brightened, and if they were lucky, the sun would come out. Two men were putting up the tent. A tall, broad, dark-haired man turned to her. Startled, she jumped. The man looked very much like Vince Tucci. Maybe this was the man JoEllen saw.

She went over to him. "You look like someone I used to know. Do you live in the area?"

"In Portsmouth," the man said.

"Then I think a friend of mine recently saw you in a nearby bar. Is that possible?" Misty knew she was a little pushy, but she had to know.

The man shrugged. "Sure. I visited one of the bars in the next town a short time ago. Why?"

"Like I said, you look like someone I used to know but don't want to meet again. Sorry to bother you."

He grinned at her. "Hey, no bother. I own this tent company with my cousin. We cover a lot of areas. Good luck on not meeting your friend."

"Thanks." Misty forced herself to look at him. Remembering her shock at seeing him, she'd felt as if a chilly wind had arisen. But now, she wondered if she could finally put to rest her fears of Vince showing up.

Carrying her dress, Misty went into the house and stopped in the kitchen. A young woman and a man were at work setting up trays of food for the reception. She studied the platters. Cooked shrimp on top of squares of avocado toast and stuffed mushrooms were just a few of the items they were working on.

She knew cold poached salmon and beef filet with bearnaise sauce would also be served, along with a number of things she hadn't yet heard about. In addition to gourmet dinners, preparing this food was a smart way for Melissa to advertise her catering services.

Crystal was in her bathroom, waiting for Misty to help with her hair. Crystal had worn purple in her hair for years until she decided she didn't need that distraction anymore. Now, her natural blonde was lovely. Misty knew how to braid a few strands of her hair to keep her face clear of wisps and add a bit of elegance to her usual shoulder-length style.

"Are you excited?" asked Misty, hanging up her dress.

"Yes. Excited, worried, nervous," said Crystal. "The security guard should be arriving soon. I hope there won't be any trauma with Emmett's father. Weddings aren't always the best time for families, especially with someone who makes it a drama about himself."

"Having GG and all your friends surrounding you will help keep things in order. No one is going to let Emmett's father ruin this time for you," Misty said with determination she felt to her toes.

"I know, I know," said Crystal. "I want this to be perfect for Emmett and me. A day to remember."

"It'll all work out," said Misty, though she couldn't help worrying, too.

Whitney Gilford Woodruff, GG's oldest granddaughter, now married to the Chief of Police, knocked on the door and stuck her head inside. "Hi, Nick and I are here. Nick will change his clothes in one of the other bedrooms with Emmett. But when it's time, I'm going to help you two get dressed."

"Great," said Crystal. "Come downstairs with me. You can help get the tables set in the tent. The food will come out after the ceremony."

"Nick already spoke to the security guard to let him know who he was in case help was needed."

"That's great," said Misty. She couldn't shake the worrisome feeling that normal weddings didn't require a security guard.

As Misty carried tableware to the tent, the sun broke through the gray clouds, and she breathed a sigh of relief. It was a good sign.

A heavy-set, middle-aged man approached them. "Hello. I'm Ike Benson from AAA Security." He wore tan slacks, a short-sleeved button-collared shirt, and a cotton khaki vest, under which He Misty noticed a gun in a holster. "I'm here to help with the wedding."

"Trust me, it's not like a shotgun wedding," said Crystal. "The groom's father is well-known, and we want to keep news people and photographers away. The groom's father doesn't know about these arrangements, and that's how we want to keep it."

Ike bobbed his head. "Understood. How many people are you expecting?"

"I'm guessing around fifty," said Crystal. "It's a surprise wedding, so people will arrive expecting a picnic. That's how we wanted it."

"Okay. The three of you women indicate who should be escorted out, and I'll take care of it," said Ike.

"Thanks," said Crystal. "By the way, the groom's stepfather is Everett Chamberlain."

Ike's eyes widened. "He's running for president, right?"

"Yes. That's the problem. He wants publicity, and my fiancé and I don't."

Ike shook his head. "Well, we can try our best to outwit the press, but it won't be easy if he's notified them. It helps that there's limited access to the backyard."

Crystal and Misty exchanged worried looks.

"My husband, Nick, whom you just met, will try to help," said Whitney. "He's the local police chief."

"Say, aren't you that actress?" said Ike.

Surprised, Whitney was gracious. "Yes, but I'm not working at the moment."

"Okay, then, let's get the show on the road," said Ike. "I'll set up my station near the entrance by the driveway and keep an eye on the people coming in."

Whitney placed a hand on Crystal's arm. "Nick has arranged for one of his deputies to help Ike. Between the two of them, they ought to be able to do as you want."

The minister of the local Unitarian church came over to them. "I'm a few minutes late, but I see we have plenty of time."

"Yes," said Crystal. "The flowers are just arriving now."

A staff member from Petals was carrying a gorgeous arrangement of summer flowers in a large white wicker basket for the buffet table. "I've got the bride's and maid of honor's flowers in the truck."

Curious, Misty went over to the truck and gasped with delight when she saw the same multi-colored summer flowers in two separate bouquets and a flower ring, like a crown, to be placed on Crystal's head.

She turned to Crystal. "These are stunning."

Crystal looked pleased. "They turned out so well."

"You'd better go in and change," said Whitney. "I see people are starting to arrive. Don't worry about Emmett and Nick. I'll see that they go inside. Dani and Brad are bringing GG, and Taylor will keep an eye out for Natalie."

"What would I do without the Gilford girls?" said Crystal, hugging Whitney.

Misty followed Crystal inside and up to her bedroom.

Nick and Emmett followed.

Outside Crystal's bedroom door, Emmett stopped to give her a kiss.

"Remember, the groom can't see the bride's dress before it's time," Misty said, thinking Emmett was adorable with Crystal.

"Okay, then, see you two outside," said Emmett. "Nick and I will be ready."

Misty noticed Nick was wearing tan slacks and a crisp white shirt. A blue blazer, she knew, would be added, and at Emmett's request, neither man would be wearing a tie.

Inside the bedroom, Misty slipped on her dress and twirled around for Crystal.

"It's lovely. All the right colors. You look smashing in it," said Crystal. "Now, please help me with mine."

Crystal pulled a midi-length white silk dress from the closet. Simple, it had a V-neckline, capped sleeves, a fitted bodice, and a skirt that fell straight down and flowed with movement. Crystal slipped on the dress, and it fit her like a glove.

Observing her sister in this stunning dress, Misty felt unexpected tears. "My God! You're beautiful."

"Thanks," said Crystal. She turned at the sound of a knock on the door. "That must be the photographer with Captured Moments. She promised to take photographs of us getting ready."

Crystal opened the door, and a young woman with a turquoise streak of color in her dark-brown hair beamed at them, lighting her blue-green eyes. Fairly new to town, she was trying to make a go of her photography studio. Misty had seen some of her work and was impressed.

"Hi, ladies. It looks like you're almost ready. I'm glad I got here in time to get some photos of you. You both look stunning. Now, show me some sisterly love so I can capture it."

Misty put her arm around Crystal, careful not to crush her dress. She had only to think of how much Crystal meant to her to bring a genuine, loving smile to her face.

"Excellent," said the photographer. "I'll take a few of you, Misty, helping to place Crystal's flowers on her head."

She took a few more photos of them and said, "I'm going outside to capture the surprise on some of the people's faces when they realize a wedding is happening."

"Please send up Whitney," said Crystal. "I want to get an update from her."

Moments later, Whitney appeared in Crystal's bedroom.

"How are things going?" Crystal asked.

"The only person not here is Emmett's stepfather. All our friends have arrived except for Nettie and Jason, who are on the way. GG and Natalie are sitting and talking together and seem to be having fun."

"Is the security guard checking everyone?" Crystal asked.

"Yes. I understand he spoke to the photographer when she arrived with her cameras, but there's been no sign of any other media people. I think it's safe to say that if Emmett's stepfather does show up, he'll be quickly controlled. The security guard has been doing an excellent job."

"Okay, this waiting is killing me," said Crystal. "Will you please ask the guitar player to start the music Emmett and I chose? The longer we wait, the more trouble might come from Everett. And please tell Emmett and Nick to go ahead and take their places. When I hear my song being played, I'll send Misty outside, and I'll follow."

Whitney left, and Crystal turned to Misty. "I'm not about to wait for Everett. He knew what time the wedding would begin. It's just like him to be late so he can make a grand entrance."

"Will Emmett be sorry about Everett not seeing the two of you get married?" asked Misty.

Crystal shook her head. "Sadly, no. Emmett's pretty upset about the way his stepfather is treating this event. He feels it's disrespecting both of us."

"All right. I'm going to make a quick trip to the bathroom, then go downstairs to wait for your signal," said Misty.

Misty waited for Crystal to appear in the kitchen, nervously shifting from one foot to the other.

She heard her approaching, and when she saw her sister arrive looking angelic in her white dress and wearing a floral crown like a halo around her beautiful face, tears stung Misty's eyes. Crystal was such a special person; she deserved a lovely wedding without any shenanigans from her future father-in-law.

"Ready?" Crystal asked her.

Misty kissed Crystal's cheek. "You're lovely. Let's make this happen."

Crystal stood aside while Misty stepped outside onto the lawn and headed toward the minister, Emmett, and Nick. She heard the gasps of admiration from the crowd at seeing Crystal behind her, and her smile widened. As she entered the circle of friends gathered for the wedding, she caught David's eye, and her heart fluttered. Maybe, thought Misty, someday she'd be as lucky as Crystal.

The minister kept the traditional wedding service short, as promised. By the time Crystal and Emmett had said their vows to one another, there wasn't a dry eye in the gathering, including Natalie's. Their sweet words to one another resonated with the crowd.

Just as the minister announced, "You may now kiss your bride," David came up beside Misty and squeezed her hand, giving her a sweet smile.

A commotion broke out by the house. The entire group turned and faced Everett and his entourage. Everett's loud, booming voice rang out. "What do you mean I can't attend my son's wedding? This is an important occasion for me as father of the groom."

Ike Benson stood squarely in front of the senator. "Hold on. I'll have to have permission for you to enter. The photographer and news person aren't allowed at this event."

Furious, Everett shook his fist at him. "I'll be damned if I'm going to let you keep me from my family." He stopped talking when Emmett walked over to him.

"So, you've come to congratulate Crystal and me?" said Emmett calmly, coolly. "The ceremony is over, but you're welcome to help us celebrate privately, without cameras and newspeople. I explained that to you yesterday. Why are you late getting here?"

Everett looked down at the ground and shuffled his feet. "The traffic was bad."

"Traffic in Lilac Lake?" scoffed Emmett as Crystal, Misty, and Nick approached.

"I was doing an interview in Boston," Everett admitted, tugging at the collar of his white shirt.

Emmett let out a long sigh. "I wish I could say that this kind of behavior was unusual, gentlemen," he said to Everett's handlers. "But, as you well know, it isn't. I suggest you find something to do while my stepfather enjoys some time here. Unless he chooses not to."

Everett held up his hand. "Now, Emmett, you know I'll do no such thing. It's family time. And this is a big celebration." He turned to the members of his entourage. "Excuse me. I'll see you later. There's a nice café in town. I'll meet you there."

No one in the wedding party corrected Everett. The café had closed for the wedding. That's the kind of town Lilac Lake was and how respected Crystal and Emmett were.

CHAPTER EIGHTEEN

MISTY AND THE OTHER WOMEN IN THE GROUP SURROUNDED Crystal as Everett entered the backyard. They'd been delighted and excited by the unexpected wedding and stood by, admiring Crystal's dress and asking questions about the honeymoon.

Beaming, Crystal said, "The honeymoon is a surprise for me. Emmett has told me to pack lightly, and I know we'll be going out to dinner. That's it."

Hazel walked over to Misty. "You sure know how to keep a secret. This wedding is lovely. How long have you known about it?"

"Not that long," Misty said, amused. "But I'm relieved I won't have to keep that secret anymore."

"You look great," said Hazel, moving back as Everett approached the group.

"Ah, here's the bride," he boomed. "Welcome to the family. Such a beautiful addition."

Crystal's lips curved, but Misty could tell her smile was forced.

Emmett hurried over and put an arm around Crystal. "It didn't take me long to realize this was the woman I wanted to spend the rest of my life with."

"I will be proud to introduce her and you, of course, Emmett, to my constituents."

Emmett shook his head. "That's not going to happen. I've chosen to stay out of the limelight, and Crystal agrees with me."

"That's right," said Crystal. "But we wish you luck with your campaign."

Everett frowned. "We'll talk later. This is about you and your wedding. Again, I'm sorry I missed the ceremony."

Jason, a chef and one of the new owners of the café, came over to them holding a tray of tulip glasses filled with champagne. Misty noticed Melissa had another such tray.

"Please help yourself to one," said Jason. "Nick is about to give a toast to the bride and groom."

Misty took one and moved with the others toward Nick, who was waiting for them to join him. Crystal and Emmett had moved beside him.

When it was quiet, Nick held up his glass. "Here's to the bride and groom, a wonderful couple who are very much a part of this community. You all know how special Crystal is to me, and what you don't know, perhaps, is that Emmett and I spend some free time together fishing. I won't say who the better fisherman is except to tell you that Whitney is getting very good at frying up fresh fish for dinner."

When the laughter subsided, Nick continued. "We wish you both the best of everything to come. I think it's fair for me to speak for all of us gathered here when I say that you both are beloved in this community. Here's to Crystal and Emmett!"

Misty raised her glass with the others and turned to David, who'd come up beside her.

"You look beautiful," he said softly into her ear.

Tingles of pleasure filled her. It was an emotional time for her, and hearing his compliment meant a lot to her. She gazed up at him, and from the look he gave her, she wasn't surprised when he brushed his lips against her cheek in a gentle sweep.

Her attention was drawn away from him when Everett moved to stand by Nick and held up his glass. "I'd like to say a few words if you'll allow it." His confident manner indicated he'd naturally assumed they'd be honored to hear from him.

Everett clapped a hand on Emmett's back. "This young man has been part of my life since he was a toddler and is a son that I'm proud to call my own. He may have chosen to be a doctor here in this town, but he's an important member of the family his mother and I have made together. So, it will come as no surprise when I announce to all who know me how delighted I am now to have a daughter to add to the clan."

Misty could see Emmett's jaw clenching and unclenching and knew how agitated he was. Emmett had changed his name from Chamberlain to Chambers to avoid being known as the senator's son, needing to strike out on his own. He'd made it clear to Crystal that he wanted no part of his stepfather's campaign. They both agreed it was best to keep it that way.

Now, Everett was trying to change things.

Crystal placed a hand on Emmett's arm. "Thank you, Everett. Please enjoy the food and drinks, everyone. There's plenty for all."

Misty headed to the buffet table to fix herself a plate of food. Melissa, Nettie, and Jason had done a fantastic job with it. Everything looked beautiful, with each platter displaying a garnish of fresh herbs or flowers.

She helped herself to a small taste of everything and moved to one of the benches in the yard. Taylor was taking food to GG and Natalie sitting together in chairs under the shade of a tree.

"May I join you?" asked David.

She patted the space next to her, and after he sat down, they both smiled and posed for the woman who was circulating, taking shots of the guests.

Nearby, Everett said to the photographer, "May I ask you to take a photo of me with the bride and groom?"

"Of course," she answered politely. She gave Misty an apologetic look and walked away, with Everett following her.

David shook his head. "I don't blame Emmett for wanting to distance himself from his stepfather. He seems such a self-centered, egotistical man. I talked to Emmett's mother, and she was pleasant in comparison."

"But still not warm," said Misty. "Crystal is healthy for Emmett."

David gave her a thoughtful look and nodded.

"Can I join you?" asked Hazel.

Soon, a group had gathered on the lawn around them.

"Seems everyone has made it here," said David, gazing around.

"Even JoEllen," said Misty, shaking her head as she watched JoEllen flirt with Everett. He, of course, seemed to love it.

After she had finished eating, Misty tossed her plastic plate and utensils into a trash can by the tent and walked over to check on GG and Natalie, who seemed to be congenial.

"Is there anything I can get for you?" Misty asked them.

"No, thank you. I'm saving room for dessert," said GG.

"Melissa told us about the lemon and berry layered cake she'd made," Natalie said.

"It's got to be delicious. If this reception is any indication of how gourmet meals are going to be, they're sure to be a success," said Misty. She pulled a chair up to them.

GG beamed at her. "It's been a lovely wedding. And you, my dear, look beautiful."

"I saw you with your young man," commented Natalie.

Heat flushed Misty's cheeks. She didn't know how to respond.

"David and Misty are friends," said GG. A sparkle entered her eyes. "But time may make a change to that."

Chuckling, Misty stood. "You're incorrigible, GG." She bent

down and kissed her cheek. "I'd better go see if I can help."

"Such a wonderful young woman," Misty heard GG say as she left them, and her vision blurred. She loved the phrase, "It takes a village to raise a child." In her case, it was very true.

As it grew dark, Crystal and Emmett went into the house to change clothes and returned dressed casually.

"Okay, let the party begin," said Emmett. He'd arranged for speakers to be set up outside, and music rocked the air of the backyard. Guests began dancing with one another.

Everett and Ike, the security guard, had already left. Misty and David offered to give Natalie a ride back to the Inn. Cooper had already left with GG.

Misty held her breath as David helped Natalie into his truck. It seemed incongruous to see stiff, formal Natalie in the passenger seat, but she didn't seem at all fazed by it.

And later, with Misty seated behind her, Natalie opened up a bit. "I'm sorry that Everett was late to the ceremony. I wish I could agree with him that his campaign comes first, but I can't. His ambition has always been like a woodlands creature too restless to capture."

"That must be difficult to handle," said Misty. "I understand why Emmett chose not to get involved. How are you going to deal with it going forward?"

"Like always, I'll support him because I think he makes a difference for people. Unfortunately, it's at a personal loss."

Misty was surprised by Natalie's frankness, but sitting with GG for hours may have played a part. GG didn't accept any excuses from anyone. Discussions with her were always honest.

By the time Misty and David returned to Emmett's house, things were winding down. The backyard was cleaned up, and the only music playing now was soft and low.

"I'm going to say goodbye to Crystal and Emmett, and then I'm going home. Would you like to stop by for a cold drink before heading across the lake to your place?" Misty asked David.

"Yes. I'm not sure what you have planned for the rest of the weekend, but I hope you'll come to my cabin for dinner tomorrow," said David.

"Okay, that'll be nice," Misty said. "And then we're both invited to the picnic at the Lilac Lake Cottage. It'll be the last busy weekend of the summer."

"Do you want to ride in my truck to your house?" David asked.

"Thanks, but I'd better drive my car. I don't have to worry about picking it up from here tomorrow."

As they approached her cabin in the dark, Misty glanced in her rearview mirror at David's truck behind her. She was grateful he wanted to make sure she was safe. Her security system helped make her feel protected, but after seeing David making his karate moves, she felt even safer.

Sugar's barks could be heard before they even reached the front door.

"Guess she takes her job seriously," said David.

"She's sweet with others but a real watchdog at home," said Misty.

Misty opened the door and punched in the code for the security system. Sugar wiggled with happiness at seeing them. Misty picked her up and hugged her as she walked to the kitchen. She checked to make sure Sugar had eaten, and her water bowl still had plenty.

She opened the sliding door for Sugar and turned on the outside lights. "It's still a lovely evening outside," she said to David. "What can I get you to drink?"

"How about a cold glass of water?" said David.

"I can do that," Misty said, giving him a wide smile. Being with him was just what she needed after such an eventful day. "I'll be right back."

She filled two glasses with ice water, grabbed an envelope from her purse, and returned to the deck.

"Here you go," she said, handing him his water. "Now, I get to see where Emmett is taking Crystal for their honeymoon." She set down her glass and held up an envelope. "Emmett put the information inside here and wouldn't say anything about it to anyone but his replacement for fear his surprise would be ruined. But he wanted someone in the family to know where they'd be for emergency purposes."

She opened the envelope, stared at the words, and let out a whoop of joy. "Paris! They're going to Paris! I'm so excited for Crystal. It's something she's always wanted to do."

David grinned. "Nice."

Misty folded the paper and set it aside. "Let's toast to that!" She raised her glass, and playing along, David clicked his glass against hers.

"How did you think everything at the wedding went?" Misty asked him. "Emmett's father is something else. As nice as everything turned out, I know Crystal is relieved to have the wedding behind her."

"Senator Everett Chamberlain is a first-class jerk," said David. "He makes me realize how lucky I am with my parents. Emmett is a strong guy, perfect for Crystal."

"I think so, too," said Misty, letting out a sigh of appreciation. Sugar came up to her, and Misty stroked her soft curls, loving the feel of them. She gazed over at David, and a sense of peace filled her. She couldn't help wondering how their relationship would continue to grow.

"Thanks for the drink," said David, standing. "I have to be up early for a project with the new owners of a house in The Woods. But tomorrow night, there will be no such curfew."

He held out his hand, and she took it.

Standing in front of him, seeing the flush of his cheeks as he gave her a sexy look, Misty's heart raced. She pushed away thoughts of how big, how tall, how strong he seemed and closed her eyes in time for his lips to meet hers.

A thread of heat burned its way through her, filling her with desire. He pulled her closer, and she moved against him, trying to forget Vince's arms around her, holding her too tight.

David lifted her chin and stared into her eyes. "It's all right. You're shivering."

Tears filled her eyes. "I'm sorry."

"Don't be," he said and gently wiped a tear from her cheek. "Let's just think of this as practicing, allowing you to become used to me, to us."

"I like that," she said and forced a smile though her heart was pounding.

He lowered his lips to hers once more, and this time, she thought only of him.

CHAPTER NINETEEN

THE NEXT MORNING, MISTY SAT WITH HAZEL IN HER kitchen, rehashing the wedding.

"I'm relieved for Crystal that Emmett doesn't want to be part of all the campaigning. It makes her life much easier. Emmett's father is someone I wouldn't want to spend a lot of time with." Hazel shook her head. "But he didn't ruin the wedding, after all. In a way, it's best he wasn't there for the ceremony, which was so sweet."

"I agree," said Misty. "Emmett is a great guy. Thoughtful too. I can only imagine the joy on Crystal's face when she learns they're flying to Paris for their honeymoon. She's wanted to go there forever."

"Just think of all the beautiful art, clothes, and fashion," said Hazel. "I've been to England but not to France."

"Crystal has wanted to travel there for the food," said Misty. "Let's hope she comes back with some great ideas for the gourmet dinners she and Melissa will put on."

"Speaking of food, I've ordered a picnic from the café to take with us for our canoe trip on the lake," said Hazel. "I figured we'd need it. Especially after celebrating at the wedding."

"I was too busy keeping watch over everything to do much eating or drinking," said Misty. "I couldn't let Emmett's parents ruin Crystal's wedding. Thankfully, Emmett's mother was as determined as I to see that Everett behaved."

Hazel made a face. "Guess you didn't see this in the online news." She handed her phone to Misty.

The headline read: "Senator Everett Chamberlain takes time from a busy schedule to help celebrate his son's wedding." Beneath it was a photo of the Senator with his arms around Emmett and Crystal.

Misty felt her cheeks heat with anger. "That slime! I hope neither Crystal nor Emmett see this. He must've bribed the photographer into giving him the photo he asked her to take."

Hazel placed a hand on Misty's arm. "It just proves what an ass he is. I wouldn't worry about it. Emmett and Crystal are, hopefully, having too much fun on their way to Paris to care."

"You're right. It's useless to worry about it. Are you sure you don't mind if Sugar comes with us?"

Hazel shook her head. "It'll be fine. Let's go. We'll stop at the Café on our way."

When they got to The Meadows clubhouse at the end of the lake, a lot of activity was taking place. Many of the canoes from the storage rack were missing, and someone had brought a paddle boat and tied it to the dock. Adults and kids were swimming in the designated area or sitting on a small beach. Sugar was curious about all of it.

Hazel held up the set of keys Dani had given her and pulled a piece of paper out of her pocket. "I've got the instructions. They're pretty simple. Dani's canoe is green. And she's given me a number for her locker."

They unlocked the canoe from the rack and then took out the lifejackets, paddles, and cushions from the locker. As they were walking to the edge of the water, Misty heard a child crying and turned to see Brody huddled in the sand. A large man stood over him, talking loud enough for Misty to hear.

Listening to the man, who obviously was Brody's father, berate him for being afraid to go into the water, Misty's stomach curled. She walked over to them.

"Hi, Brody!" she smiled at him and turned to his father. "Hello. I'm Misty Owens, Brody's teacher. It's nice to meet you. Is there a problem?"

Brody's father made a face. "Harley Kirk. Brody is being his usual self and doesn't want to try something new. It's a great day to be in the water."

"Have you gone in with him?" Misty asked Harley.

"No, I'm sitting with a bunch of guys over there." He indicated a group of workmen sitting under the shade of a tree several yards away.

"Is there any other family here?"

Harley shook his head. "No, I'm a single father. I try my best, but like I told him, Brody is just a chicken at heart. He never wants to do anything."

Misty reminded herself to speak calmly. "He might need to get used to the water. Can he swim?"

"Not yet. Ain't gonna happen if he doesn't try."

"Why don't you help him get used to the water and go from there?"

Harley's brown eyes flashed with anger. "Yeah? Why don't you mind your own business? He's my kid, and he'll do what he's told." He turned to Brody. "You stay here. I'm going with my friends."

Sugar growled and sat by Brody.

Brody did his best to hide his face, but Misty could see wetness on his cheeks. She longed to pick him up and hug him. Instead, not wanting to increase his father's anger, she sat down on the sand beside him. "It's okay, Brody. It takes some of us a while to get used to a new idea. Even if you don't go into the water, you can get your feet wet at the edge of it. Maybe even build something with the sand. Would you like that?"

Brody shrugged, still keeping his face averted. They both looked up as his father approached.

"I told you to mind your own business," Harley said to her forcefully. "C'mon, Brody, we have to go."

"It'll be all right," Misty told Brody, giving him a hopeful smile. But inside, her pulse was racing so hard she thought she might collapse. She knew she'd have to tread carefully. But if that man spoke to Brody like that in public, she could imagine what he was like in the privacy of their home.

She placed a hand on Brody's thin shoulder. "I'll see you at school on Tuesday."

Brody studied the ground.

As Brody's father strode away, making it difficult for Brody to keep up, Misty turned away from them, and her distress grew. Sugar, sensing her unhappiness, stayed by her side.

Hazel hurried over to her. "What's the matter? Is that the student you were worried about?"

Unable to speak, Misty unclenched her fists. She felt so damned helpless. Things in that household weren't right, and she was worried. Brody was a little boy who didn't seem to have anyone to talk to. She'd speak to the school counselor about it.

"I'm really concerned," Misty said and drew a deep breath to calm herself. "Okay, let's go."

They got the canoe into the water and loaded it with their picnic and equipment. With Hazel sitting in the bow and Sugar in the middle, Misty pushed the canoe out onto the surface of the lake and quickly hopped in, rocking the canoe a bit.

Sugar yapped and then quieted as Misty began talking to her. Misty was thrilled for her presence. She was sure if Brody's father had attacked her physically, Sugar would've reacted.

Out on the water, they took some time coordinating strokes. Misty used her position in the stern to guide the canoe while Hazel paddled and pulled in the water consistently.

"I thought we could picnic at the Lilac Lake Cottage," said Hazel.

"I've got a better idea. David's parents own a cottage across the lake from the Inn. It would be a perfect place to set up a picnic on the shoreline. I know they wouldn't mind, and it would give us more room with the dog."

"Okay, let's do it," said Hazel. "How much farther? My arms are aching already."

Misty chuckled. "Keep going. Paddling a canoe isn't as easy as it looks sometimes."

The sun beat down on them and glistened off the water. Misty gave Sugar some water and took some sips herself. The heat didn't bother her, especially because she could detect something in the air that smelled of autumn to her. And she knew that fall and then winter would be here all too soon. As much as some in their group enjoyed winter sports, Misty preferred the summer months.

They passed the Inn, Lilac Lake Cottage, and the end of the lake, where ducks swam among the reeds, before heading up the other side of the lake.

She was as relieved as Hazel when the Grahams' dock appeared. No one was sitting on it.

Misty guided the canoe to the side of the dock and turned to Hazel. "Wait here. I'll go check to see if anyone is home. I'm sure it's okay, but I want to ask for permission, if possible."

Misty climbed out of the canoe and told Sugar to stay. Whining, the dog did as she was told.

"I'll keep her here," said Hazel. "Go ahead."

Misty climbed the wooden stairs to the front of the house and knocked on the door.

When Susie answered, Misty was pleased to see her face light with pleasure at the sight of her.

"Misty! Nice to see you."

"My friend Hazel and I are wondering if we could have a picnic on your shoreline. We have Sugar with us, and I thought it would be easier away from everyone else."

"By all means, you're welcome to set up on any part of the shore. You may use the dock if you prefer."

"Thank you, but we'll sit in the shade on the shore. We've had enough sun," said Misty.

"Then, help yourselves. I may come down to say hello in a while. I've got a cake baking in the oven and can't leave until it's done."

"Okay. I want to introduce you to Hazel. She's new in town and teaches with me at the elementary school."

"Lovely. I'll see you soon."

Misty and Hazel spread a blanket on the ground beneath a tree and opened the picnic basket Nettie had given them. As curious as she was about the food, Sugar caught sight of a squirrel and took off running.

Chuckling, Misty turned to Hazel. "Guess Sugar will stay busy." She leaned forward to peer into the basket. "What did Nettie pack for us?"

"A feast," said Hazel. "I see deviled eggs, sliced tomatoes, a green salad, and a couple of sandwiches." She started laying the dishes on top of the blanket. "There are cookies, too."

Misty opened a can of soda and took a long sip. "That tastes delicious after working hard."

She helped herself to an egg and then took a bite of salad. Both Hazel and she had been quiet as they paddled. Being out on the water, moving smoothly through it was humbling. She thought of native tribes traveling like this many years ago and realized what a precious thing it was to enjoy nature. Now, looking out at the water and the Inn on the other side of the lake, she felt a peacefulness fill her.

"It's nice that Mrs. Graham allows us to use their property like this," said Hazel. "You're lucky, Misty, that she likes you so much. That's one of my problems with the man my mother would love me to marry back home. His mother is nice to me, but we don't have a warm relationship."

"Oh, that's too bad," said Misty.

"In truth, I think Ron is a bit of a mama's boy," said Hazel. "There's more to it than that, but it's another reason I'm not interested in him." She indicated the area around them. "Here, I feel free to be myself."

"In the end, that's all you can be," said Misty. "And, Hazel,

I'm very happy you're here."

"Me, too," said Hazel, beaming at her.

They looked up as Susie Graham approached. "I hope you saved some room for a piece of warm carrot cake. It is a favorite of my men."

"A favorite of mine, too," said Misty. "Come sit with us." She patted a place on the blanket next to her. "Susie, this is my friend, Hazel Belmont. Hazel, this is Susie Graham."

"Lovely to meet you, Hazel." Smiling with pleasure, Susie handed her the plate with two pieces of cake and lowered herself to the blanket. "It's good to see you, Misty. What's new?"

"Did you hear about the wedding?" Misty asked. "Crystal looked like a golden angel."

"You'll have to show me pictures when you get them," said Susie. "When he stopped by to talk to his dad about the business, David mentioned something about Emmett's father showing up late."

Misty and Hazel filled Susie in on all the details and Susie, like many others, agreed Senator Chamberlain was a jerk.

"And guess what? Emmett surprised Crystal with a trip to Paris for their honeymoon," said Misty.

"Rod and I went to Paris for our twentieth anniversary, and it was so much fun. Delicious too. We went to a couple of fancy restaurants that still are my favorite meals."

Misty knew Rod and David worked hard with the landscaping business, digging and sweating as they completed their jobs. So, an image of Rod eating in restaurants in Paris seemed incongruous. But she loved the idea.

During the course of the conversation, Misty brought up seeing Brody and his father. "Seeing Brody cry while his father called him names, my heart went out to him. I tried to talk to Brody's father, but he got mad at me and told me to mind my own business. The whole situation is very wrong."

"Where was Brody's mother?" asked Susie.

"Apparently, she's out of the picture. Brody's father, Harley, told me he's a single dad." Misty sighed. "I feel helpless, and yet, when I see and hear what's happening, it makes me sick."

Susie reached over and patted her hand. "I understand, but be careful when dealing with a parent's handling of his child. But, as we've talked about, you need to keep an eye on Brody. And certainly, if any physical signs of abuse or neglect are apparent, you must report it to the authorities."

They talked of other things. Then, with Sugar panting beside her, Misty said, "We probably should head back. Thank you, Susie, for letting us picnic here."

"It's my pleasure," said Susie, standing. "It's always a pleasure to see you." She accepted the empty plate she was given and headed toward the house.

"Susie's cool," said Hazel, carrying the basket to the canoe.

"Yes, she is," Misty said, realizing once more how lucky she was to have such a warm, caring woman in her life.

#

That evening, David picked Misty up for dinner. "Sugar can come with us. It'll be good for her to get out of the house."

"She was running around your parents' house chasing squirrels when Hazel and I stopped there for a picnic on their property. Your mother gave us warm pieces of her carrot cake," said Misty. "It was delicious."

"It's one of my favorites." He waited while she set the alarm and locked up. Then, he helped both Misty and Sugar into his truck.

"Do you have tomorrow off work?" she asked.

"Yes. Finally," said David. "It's been a real Labor Day weekend for me. This is when people realize what work they want done before winter."

"I understand. It's as if autumn is suddenly here, and winter is not far behind."

"It'll be nice to relax and enjoy the day."

"We have more and more people in our group," said Misty. "It makes it fun."

"I like it too," said David. "I'm especially glad you came back to Lilac Lake." He gave her hand a squeeze.

"Me too," she said, satisfied she was moving forward with her life.

They'd just arrived at David's house when the neighbor's dog, Homer, appeared. Sugar and Homer touched noses and, tails wagging, started to chase one another around. Misty was proud of the way Sugar handled herself with the black lab, who was much bigger.

Chuckling to herself, she wondered if it was parental pride to feel that way.

David led Misty into the house. "Let's let the dogs work off some of that energy before coming into the house."

In the kitchen, David offered her a glass of wine. "Sorry, I didn't have time to do anything fancy. I picked up a cooked chicken and some other stuff for dinner. I hope you don't mind."

"Not at all," said Misty. "It's nice to be out of the house and not to have to worry about a meal. I'll help you put this together."

David studied her. "You're such a great person."

"Thanks," said Misty, knowing it sounded lame, but she couldn't remember Vince ever saying that to her.

"I mean it," said David softly, drawing her into his arms.

Everything felt right with David. She gazed up at him and closed her eyes as his lips met hers. It was never like this with Vince.

When they pulled apart, they both were smiling.

Homer barked to come inside. David opened the door, and both dogs came in.

Sugar came right over to Misty and, panting, sat at her feet.

Misty laughed at her. "You've had more exercise in one day than in maybe forever."

"It's good for her," said David. "Want to watch the sunset from the porch?"

"Yes. I love this time of day."

The four of them moved to the porch, and while the adults sank into chairs, the two dogs flopped on the floor.

Misty enjoyed the quiet moments that she and David shared, watching the colors in the sky change from orange to pale yellow and finally gray. She usually used this time for reflection and found her thoughts returning to him and how his kiss had made her both excited and calm, as if she was where she was supposed to be.

As if he sensed her feelings, he reached over and took hold of her hand, letting his smile speak for him.

She returned it, aware of how special this moment was.

They enjoyed another small glass of wine and then went inside. While David carved the chicken, Misty put together a green salad and set out the potato salad David had bought.

They sat at the kitchen table and helped themselves to food. After working hard all day, David proved he needed a substantial amount of it.

They cleaned up the kitchen and relaxed on the couch. Sugar fitted herself between them and snored softly as they watched a suspense movie that forced Misty to close her eyes from time to time.

"That was great," said David when it ended.

"Scary," Misty commented. "I'm lucky I have Sugar to keep me company at home."

They both looked at the dog sleeping on her back, oblivious to the world and couldn't help laughing.

"I think the security system is a little safer for you," said David. He stood and pulled her to her feet. They stood staring at one another. David's steady look sent heat through her, and she knew he wanted to kiss her. She lifted up on her toes and sighed as he brought his lips to hers.

David glanced at the bedroom door and said, "Guess I'd better get you home."

"Yes, it's been a long day. A lovely one." She knew he wanted more from her but wouldn't push until she was ready.

CHAPTER TWENTY

THE NEXT MORNING, MISTY LAY IN BED THINKING OF Crystal, hoping she was having a fabulous time in Paris. Her thoughts drifted to David and his family. She was falling hard for him, but she wouldn't tell him until she was more confident in herself. She realized her feelings for David included loving his family, which made it more complicated.

She got up and dressed for her morning walk through town.

"Ready for a walk?" Misty asked Sugar, and Sugar came running to her. Misty hooked a leash to her harness, locked up the house, and headed out. Sugar knew exactly where they were going and led the way. It was cool, a reminder of days to come, and Misty enjoyed the briskness of their pace. If she looked carefully, she could see subtle changes to the leaves. Gone was the early bright green of spring. A faint yellow had entered some leaves as if readying to show off brighter colors in a month or so. She saw a flash of red and smiled as a cardinal took flight. It was a good omen, signaling a nice day ahead.

As they entered the park, Misty saw David's father. He was kneeling in front of one of the flower beds, pulling weeds.

Tears stung her eyes at how carefully he worked among the flowers, seeing the work as a tribute to his daughter.

Sugar pulled so hard on her leash that it slipped out of Misty's hands. David's father looked up and burst out laughing as the dog bounded toward him.

"Hey, Sugar," he said, getting to his feet and patting her.

Misty came over to them. "She couldn't stand not being able to greet you."

"It's great to see her. You, too. Happy Labor Day!" His deep-blue eyes, like David's, filled with light as he grinned at her.

"And to you," she said. "Hopefully, it will be a relaxing one for you. David says this is a busy time for the business."

"It's busy most of the year, until our winter break," said David's father. "Then, Susie and I will take off for Florida for a month or so."

"Susie told me you took her to Paris for an anniversary trip," said Misty. "That's where Crystal and Emmett are celebrating their honeymoon."

"I heard about their wedding. Congratulations to you for being a part of it." He stood, and Misty decided to move on so he could get back to work.

"Thanks. I'll see you later," she said, picking up the leash and leading Sugar out of the park, aware his eyes were on her.

At the Lilac Lake Café, things were busy. Dogs were

allowed on the concrete patio, so Misty headed there and was delighted to see Sarah Bullard Miller sitting at one of the tables with her twin daughters. After her husband's death, Sarah's parents, who owned the hardware store, convinced Sarah to move back to town. Sarah enjoyed a hearty laugh, was well-liked and joined the group at Jake's when she could. But helping at the store and taking care of her girls kept her busy.

Sarah waved. "You're welcome to join us." She turned to the girls. "Emily and Mia, please say hello to Ms. Owens. She teaches second grade at the school where you're attending kindergarten."

They gave her identical smiles, but one girl had light-brown hair, and the other had blond hair. All four eyes were the same attention-getting green color.

Sugar sat between their chairs and loved it when the girls stroked her.

Misty lowered herself into a chair opposite Sarah. "I'm glad you were able to make it to the wedding."

"Such a sweet, short ceremony," Sarah said. "I'm happy for Crystal. She and Emmett are a wonderful couple. Where did they go on their honeymoon? I know it was a secret."

"Paris," said Misty, grinning. "It's always been a dream of hers to go."

"What a fantastic surprise," said Sarah.

A waitress brought food for Sarah and the girls, and Misty placed an order for herself.

As she waited for her food, Misty observed Sarah's handling of the giggly girls. She seemed so calm. No wonder Aaron Collister had spent time talking to her at the wedding.

Misty's food arrived, and they all finished their meals at the same time. Misty stood. "See you later at the picnic at the cottage. I will bring brownies, but I need to get home to make them."

On the way out of the restaurant, Misty waved at Nettie.

That afternoon, after saying goodbye to Sugar, Misty drove to the Lilac Lake Cottage with a platter of warm brownies. She'd also brought lemonade to share and decided at the last minute to bring her bathing suit and a towel. For large parties like this, two bedrooms in the cottage were available for those wanting to change clothes.

She found a place to park and walked into the front yard to see it teeming with people. Like other Labor Day parties here, people came and went whenever they wanted. She saw Hazel talking to Mike and checked to see where David was. She'd parked her car near his truck.

He looked up at her and smiled as she walked toward him. "Hi. I made brownies. You said you liked them."

"I do. Here, let me carry your bag while you have the other things," said David.

She walked up to Taylor. "Shall I put the brownies on the dessert table?"

"Yes," said Taylor. "You can put the lemonade in the kitchen. We have paper cups and plenty of ice there. Clothing can be placed in one of the bedrooms. One is marked for 'girls,' and the other is for 'boys.'"

In the kitchen, Dani greeted her with a hug. "I'm glad you came. We need to talk. Follow me."

Dani led her into the living room, away from the other guests. "I understand you had a fight with Harley Kirk."

"Brody's father? I wouldn't call it a fight, necessarily. I have Brody in my class, and when I saw him with his father at The Meadows waterfront, I did make some suggestions to Harley about handling Brody." Misty could feel her blood pressure rise. "The man's a bully to his son. He was calling him a chicken for not going into the water. Alone."

"He and his family are new to the area. I understand his wife has been away in a treatment program, and while she's been gone, he's been raising Brody with her mother's help."

"That's no excuse for treating a child like that," said Misty.

"Of course not," said Dani. "I'm concerned for your well-being. Harley has a bruised ego and a quick temper. Not a good combination."

Misty let out a long sigh. "Thanks for letting me know."

They walked back to the kitchen together, where Misty grabbed a cup of lemonade. Her mind was still whirling with emotion as she went outside.

David met her. "Want to go sit on the rock? There's a nice breeze coming off the lake."

"Yes, I need to cool off," Misty said. She explained what was going on with Brody's father.

David frowned. "That doesn't sound good. Be careful, Misty."

Hazel came over to them. "Can I join you?"

"Sure," said Misty. "When did you arrive?"

"About an hour ago. It's great to see everyone,"

They turned at the commotion by the entrance. JoEllen had arrived with a man in tow.

Misty blinked rapidly, studying the outline and the size of the man. "That's him. Brody's dad, Harley," she said to David. "Leave it up to JoEllen to become involved in some way."

"Better to have him distracted by her than for him to pay attention to you. If what Dani said about him is true, just stay away from him." David took hold of her arm. "Let's go."

He led Misty and Hazel to the rock. Misty lowered herself to the warm surface and inhaled the lake air, feeling some of the tenseness leave her. She'd felt herself slipping back to when she'd been so inhibited by Vince, scared of doing something wrong.

Sensing her feelings, David clasped her hand and gave it a squeeze.

Misty smiled at him. He was right. This wasn't the same situation.

As luck would have it, as soon as they left the rock and were walking toward the food, JoEllen brought Harley over to them.

"David, Misty, and Hazel, I want you to meet Harley Kirk, a friend of mine." She clung to his arm. "He works on construction at The Meadows."

Harley didn't return JoEllen's adoring looks but did nod politely at them. David, Misty noted, did not offer to shake hands with Harley; he merely said hello.

Whenever she looked at Harley, she felt herself knotted up with concern for Brody.

Misty was sitting on the lawn with David and Dani, watching a badminton game going on. Harley and JoEllen were challenging Taylor and Cooper. For all her dislike of her, Misty had to admit JoEllen was quick on her feet. Though not as fast, Taylor and Cooper were better about cooperating as to who should go for the shot. And that's when the trouble started.

Harley and JoEllen bumped into one another several times, and each time, Harley became madder. At one point, he threw down his racket and walked away until JoEllen went to him and apologized. Harley, aware of a crowd now, tried to play again, but when he missed a shot, he swore and tossed his racket at JoEllen.

Cooper walked over to Harley and talked to him. Then, Harley left.

JoEllen burst into tears and went into the house.

"Okay, everyone," said Whitney. "It's dessert time, and

then David has promised to set off a few fireworks."

Misty turned to David. "You brought fireworks?"

David grinned. "Yeah. Everyone knows how much I love them. I keep them year-round for group celebrations."

Misty laughed. David was full of surprises.

As it grew dark, people sat on blankets and towels on the lawn, waiting for the fireworks down by the water. Brad helped David get them arranged for a show, and when the first one lit the sky with color, Misty clapped with the others.

She noticed Whitney had put earmuffs on her son, Timothy. He was walking now and seemed to delight in the colors. She observed the excitement on David's face and felt a surge of appreciation for him, thinking how unexpected it was that this sweet man, who tended to be quiet, loved making so much noise.

When the show was over, Misty helped with the cleanup, said goodbye to David, and then went to her car. JoEllen was standing next to it. "Do you mind taking me home? I thought Harley would come back, but he hasn't."

"Sure. Hop in. I'm going straight home because I have to teach tomorrow."

"Okay, thanks," said JoEllen, climbing into the passenger seat.

They rode home in silence. Misty forced herself not to ask about Harley, and JoEllen didn't want to talk about him or anything else.

CHAPTER TWENTY-ONE

THE NEXT MORNING, MISTY HURRIED TO GET READY FOR school and needed to pick up Hazel. Thankfully, Sugar cooperated by going outside and taking care of her business. School was beginning in earnest, and the lazy days of summer were over.

Hazel came out of her cabin and quickly got into the car. "After the picnic, a few of us went for a nightcap at Jake's. Now, I'm regretting it."

"Who went to Jake's?" Misty asked.

"Nettie and Jason, Aaron, Mike, Melissa, Ross, and me. It was fun. None of us could figure Harley Kirk out. The fact that he came to the picnic with JoEllen said a lot about both of them."

"We all saw how temperamental Brody's father is," said Misty. "I'm taking a karate lesson from David tonight. Do you want to join us?"

Hazel shook her head. "I can't. I promised Mike I'd go to dinner with him. He's here for a short time and then will go to Florida for a while to check on his tennis camp there."

"Where's he going to live when the sports center is done? Here or Florida?"

"I understand he'll be traveling back and forth. It seems like the best of both worlds," said Hazel.

They arrived at the school. Misty parked the car and walked with Hazel into the school.

As the children arrived, Misty studied their faces. Violet, the little girl who'd been kind to Brody, came up to her and handed her a note. "I made this for you."

Misty looked at the heart drawn on paper and said, "Thank you. That's a very sweet thing to do."

Violet gave her a big smile and went to her seat.

Brody sat in his chair, scowling. She tried to catch his attention, but he refused to look at her.

"' Morning, everyone! I hope you had a nice Labor Day weekend. Now it's time to get to work as second-grade students. Later, we'll talk about some of the things you did over the weekend."

She had a paper with addition and subtraction problems on their desks to assess her students' math skills. While the kids worked on it, she walked around the room to see how they were doing. Brody quickly finished his paper and sat staring out the window.

Misty walked over to check it. The answers were correct.

Violet, sitting next to Brody, smiled up at her. "I'm done, Ms. Owens."

"Very good. You two may read while we wait for everyone

to finish." Misty walked away to check on the other students.

Misty had just led her children outdoors for recess when Nolan Deere approached her. "Ms. Owens, I need to talk to you." He turned to Hazel. "Ms. Belmont, will you watch Ms. Owens' class if she isn't back before recess ends?"

"Of course," Hazel said, giving Misty a worried look.

Following the principal to her classroom, Misty felt like a naughty student who wasn't sure what she'd done.

Nolan closed the door behind them.

He studied her. "I've received a phone call from Brody Kirk's father. He's requesting his son be changed to a different teacher."

Misty felt her eyes widen.

"He mentioned that he saw you over the weekend talking to his son and felt a less personal relationship would be better for Brody."

"What did you say?" Misty asked, her heart pounding.

"I asked him to wait and see how things went, that you were the appropriate teacher for a student who is as bright as Brody."

"And?" she asked, surprised by Nolan's response.

"And he agreed to wait. But we will be forced to address the issue again if Body's father continues to be concerned. Is this the student you mentioned to me on the first day of school?"

"Yes. I've been able to observe Brody's father belittle him

and see how withdrawn he is. He's a bright boy and has a friend in class, a girl who sits next to him."

"I think you're the best placement for Brody. But if his father insists his child be moved out of the class, he will be. Is that clear?" Nolan's harsh look made her want to squirm.

Feeling sick, Misty said, "Yes."

Nolan left her classroom, and Misty's emotions were in turmoil. She'd be careful, but she wouldn't, couldn't give up protecting Brody.

At the end of the school day, the thought of a practice session with David was encouraging. That would make her feel more in control.

Misty drove Hazel home with a plan. She'd go for a walk with Sugar, have supper, and then meet David for her class with him. He was working long days to take advantage of the daylight, and that timing suited her.

Sugar, bless her heart, was so enthusiastic to see her that Misty rushed her outside and watched her run into the woods and race back to greet her. Misty was filled with gratitude. Sugar was the best thing to happen to her in a long time.

Misty decided that instead of going to town, she'd take Sugar to visit Ms. Overton. At the same time, she'd say hello to GG.

As they approached The Woodlands, Sugar straightened as if she knew who they were going to visit. After getting out of the car, Sugar tugged on the leash, anxious to get inside.

Misty went up to the reception desk and asked to see Ms. Overton.

The woman behind the desk shook her head. "I'm very sorry to tell you that she's no longer here. She died a few days ago."

Misty was so surprised she gasped. "Oh, I should've come earlier. I have her dog ..." She stopped talking and blinked back tears.

The woman gave her a sympathetic look. "It was very sweet of you to visit Ms. Overton earlier. I know how much she and the others here appreciated it. Would you be willing to have your dog visit with the people in the living room? They love it when dogs like yours stop in."

"Yes," said Misty. "And then I'd like to see Genie Wittner."

"Of course," the woman said. She took Misty's arm and led her into the living room.

"' Afternoon, everyone. We have special guests who'd like to say hello to you. This is Misty and her dog, Sugar."

Misty noticed the smiles in the room and unhooked Sugar from her leash. The dog seemed to know who needed her most and trotted to a woman who suddenly straightened in her chair and was reaching for the dog.

Sugar went to each person in the room, allowing them to pet her, and then she returned to Misty, her tongue hanging out. Misty picked her up. "Good girl. Now, let's say a quick hello to GG."

A few minutes later, with Sugar still in her arms, Misty knocked on GG's door.

"Come in," called GG.

Misty entered GG's apartment and set Sugar down on the floor. "Hi. We've come from visiting in the living room, and Sugar is exhausted. Do you mind if I get a drink of water for her?"

"Not at all." GG smiled as Sugar came over to her. "Such a sweet girl," GG crooned. She looked up. "How's the Maid of Honor doing? The wedding was lovely despite Everett Chamberlain making a complete ass of himself."

"I'm fine," said Misty, setting a bowl of water on the kitchen floor. "Can I get you anything?"

GG shook her head. "No, thanks. Dinner will be served shortly. How's school going?"

Misty sighed and took a seat in a chair next to the couch where GG was sitting. "The principal spoke to me today about a student whose father wants him out of my class. He's the same student I'm concerned is having issues at home."

GG shook her head. "I'm sorry."

"It's just the way it was handled," said Misty. "I'm struggling with the feeling of being threatened. It's something I need to work on."

"Oh, sweetie, I understand. It'll all work out the way it's meant to be. Have you heard from Crystal? I'm thrilled for her that Emmett chose to take her to Paris for their honeymoon."

"Me, too. Thank you for welcoming Natalie. It made things

pleasant for her."

GG waved away Misty's gratitude. "I'm happy I had the opportunity to get to know her better. She's not a bad sort, just controlled by her husband. I suspect that as Natalie becomes stronger, her life may change. She might even get the courage to walk away from him."

Misty was amused by GG's vehemence. No one had ever taken advantage of GG's being female. She'd always encouraged the young women in her life to be strong, to be self-reliant.

GG checked her watch. "I'm sorry, but they'll be announcing dinner soon, and I want to get my regular seat in the dining room. Do you mind walking there with me?"

"Not at all. I need to get home and grab dinner for Sugar and me."

Sugar heard her name and got to her feet, and the three of them took off.

After a light supper, Misty headed out to the karate studio. It would be healthy for her to get physical because her mind was repeating the meeting with Nolan Deere over and over. Each time, she got more frustrated.

When she arrived, David's truck was nowhere in sight. She got out of her car and went inside. A middle-aged man was working with a student in one of the small classrooms.

"Have you seen David Graham?" she asked.

The man shook his head. "He's marked out time on the schedule. He should be here soon."

"Okay, thanks." Misty went back to her car and waited for David to show up. The longer she waited, the more agitated she became. She was grumpy and didn't appreciate wasting her time.

Just as she was about to take off for home, David arrived in his truck. He saw her and hurried over to her car.

"Sorry, I'm late. I was trying to finish up a project. I should've taken the time to text you earlier, but the minutes kept ticking by."

She forced a smile. "Let's get started, if you don't mind. I have some schoolwork to do at home." She climbed out of the car and followed him inside, telling herself to brush off the day's frustrations.

Before class, facing her, David had Misty press her hands together and bow before they started. She knew it was a matter of routine and respect.

Once they started, David had her do a sequence of moves and then announced a change in plans. "Now, I'm going to pretend to attack you and show you what to do. Remember, quick action and smooth, surprising moves give you an advantage. Slice down with your hand, striking me on the arm, and if I come closer, swing around and kick me, sending me off balance. Got it?"

Misty nodded and stood quietly.

David charged her, sending Misty reeling backward,

fighting for her balance. As if he was really there, Misty could see Vince sneering at her before hitting her. She closed her eyes and took a deep breath.

"One more time," said David. "Then I'll let you go." He took hold of her arm.

His words struck a nerve, sending her whirling into her past where Vince had laughed while holding her so tight she couldn't escape, pretending to play around. She twisted away from him. "I can't do this. I have to go."

She hurried away from David and sprinted to her car.

David came to the entrance of the building and stopped, watching her as she sped out of the parking lot.

Tears of frustration blurred her vision. She slowed the car, though her heart was still racing. Present issues and past memories seemed to be piling up in her mind, making her unable to cope with the idea of any man having control over her—even someone like David.

At home, she unlocked her house and took care of the security system, furious with Vince, David, and herself, caught up in a cycle she was trying to break.

Sugar greeted her, and they both went out to the deck for fresh, cooling air.

David called her cell, but she didn't pick up. Couldn't. She had to figure out a way to separate Vince from David.

Later, when David phoned, she took the call.

"What's going on?" David asked.

"For a moment, fighting with you, I had another flashback.

I need time to myself to work on my issues," she said. "It's not your fault. It's mine." She'd thought she was doing so well, but now she knew what a disaster she was.

CHAPTER TWENTY-TWO

MISTY WAS SUBDUED AS SHE HEADED TO SCHOOL THE next day. She'd been awake most of the night, plagued by unwelcomed images. Not only those frightening memories with Vince, or the way Harley had snarled at her as if she wasn't worth normal courtesy, or Nolan's withering tone as he spoke to her. Other older memories filled her mind, images of her mother sobbing because of something a man said or the injuries that showed his anger. Now, she understood where her mother's unhappiness had been coming from, and she was determined not to fall into the same trap of loving someone who could destroy her.

Being with her students fulfilled Misty. She was able to focus on teaching them, welcoming their excitement at learning a new concept. And when she praised a child and saw the positive reaction it evoked, she was reminded how her encouragement would do much to give the students a good start moving forward. She remembered how Mrs. Walter had praised her.

She checked Brody and was pleased to see that he and Violet were maintaining their friendship, competing to see who could do the best on an assignment. Other students were finding satisfaction in being respectful to one another. Whenever possible, Misty pointed out acts of kindness and was satisfied to see that the children were responding positively to the star sticker rewards.

It was a satisfying way for the school year to begin.

On the way home from school, Hazel asked, "Are you all right? You seem down."

"I need some time to myself to work things out. I'm feeling as if my life is totally out of my control. I need to decide how I want to move forward. I'm not even sure I can have the sort of relationship I want with David, and he's the best man I've ever dated."

"Wow, that's really serious. Anything I can do to help?" said Hazel.

"No, thanks. I appreciate knowing you're here if I need you," she responded, thankful for her friendship.

The next few days were busy. Misty stayed away from Jake's and waited for Crystal and Emmett to arrive home from their honeymoon, hoping her ability to talk with her sister about their mother might help her work through her feelings.

Friday night, when Hazel asked Misty to join her at Jake's, Misty said yes. Truthfully, she was nervous about seeing David and some of the other guys in their group.

A short while later, they walked into Jake's.

Misty's eyes immediately searched for David. She was relieved he wasn't there. As her gaze swung around the group, she froze. Harley was there with JoEllen.

Though she wanted to run out of the building, she forced herself to stay. She went over to the group and found an empty chair at the opposite end of the table from Harley. Until then, he hadn't noticed her. But when he did, his glare was cold enough to freeze her to death.

Trying to ignore him, she turned to Poppy, who was sitting next to her, and asked her about her fall line of clothes for the store.

While they were busy talking, more and more people arrived, making her feel safer from the icy looks Harley kept throwing her way. When David arrived, he glanced at her before taking a seat at the second table in the group. It made Misty realize he deserved someone who didn't have her baggage.

The conversation was brisk, going from Crystal and Emmett's wedding to the upcoming community events.

"Save the date," said Melissa. "The first Saturday in October will be our first gourmet dinner. Crystal and I will put it on with Nettie and Jason's help. We'll have a beautiful fall menu."

"I'm going to be the maitre d," announced Ross, giving them a mock bow.

"He'll be the perfect host," Melissa said, smiling at him.

While Misty enjoyed the conversation, she was aware of the

two men who kept returning their gazes to her. When she could no longer stand it, Misty rose. "I'll see you all later."

Hazel gave her a questioning look.

"I'm fine," Misty said softly to her. "I'm going to walk back home. I don't want to disturb you."

"No, I'm coming with you," said Hazel, getting to her feet.

"I'm sorry," said Misty, climbing into Hazel's car. "I couldn't just sit there with Harley staring and David wondering about me."

"Is there anything I can do?" Hazel asked.

"Just continue to be my friend while I try to work things out in my mind."

"I'm here," soothed Hazel. "What about David? I know he's fallen for you. And tonight, he looked sad when he glanced your way."

"I don't want to lose him," said Misty. "But it won't feel right going forward with him if I don't take care of myself first."

"I understand," said Hazel. "I didn't like the way Harley stared at you. What is it with him and JoEllen?"

"She's making a fool of herself over him, fluttering her eyelashes, playing the coquette. It makes me sick," grumped Misty. "That's just what he wants. And what about Brody?"

"Don't go there," warned Hazel. "A single parent has the right to have some fun."

Misty sighed. "You're right. It's as if after meeting Brody, so many bad memories are coming back to me. My mother, my childhood, Vince. I can't bear the thought of Brody suffering because of circumstances he can't control. He's just a child. A bright little boy who deserves better."

"Still no physical signs of that?" asked Hazel.

Misty shook her head. "Let's talk about something else, shall we?"

Hazel grinned. "How about Gage? He's a handsome man."

"What about Mike? I think he really likes you," said Misty.

Hazel shrugged. "He spent a lot of time talking with Poppy. Even he admits he's a ladies' man. Heaven knows, he's not ready to get serious with anyone. I suspect he has a couple of girlfriends tucked away in Florida."

At home, Sugar's enthusiasm at seeing her gave Misty a lift in spirit. Rest, thinking pleasant thoughts, and maybe reading a romance novel were things she needed. Not a constant rehash of her past.

Sitting on the deck staring up at the stars, she thought of all the positive things in her life and decided that's what she'd do going forward. She'd had a bad boyfriend experience, but she'd gotten away from him and had started a new life in her hometown.

Misty worked on gratitude for the kind people in her life as she went about her domestic duties, including walks with Sugar and even practicing karate moves alone at home.

Sunday morning, Misty took her daily walk to the park before going to the Café for her usual coffee. She wasn't surprised when David's mother showed up. It was as if she had been waiting for her.

Smiling, Susie waved and walked over to where Misty was sitting on her favorite bench.

"It's nice to see you here. Enjoying the day so far?" Susie asked.

"Yes, I've grown to love this early morning hour," said Misty. "It's a quiet time to think about things."

"David mentioned you stopped karate lessons," Susie said, stroking Sugar's ears.

"It's more than that," Misty said. "I'm trying to work on a few personal issues. I'm still practicing some of the moves David showed me. That's important to me. I need to feel in control of my life."

"We'd all like that," Susie said, "but that isn't necessarily how life works. What's the real problem? Is it the issue at school?"

Misty sighed. "That's part of it. I wonder why I was ever in a place to permit Vince to enter my life. He was strong and was someone who made me feel safe until he turned on me. I can't let that ever happen to me again."

Susie studied Misty and then took hold of her hand.

Grateful for her warmth, Misty smiled and listened as Susie continued. "This is where a certain amount of awareness and faith come in. It's smart to be prepared. But you have to trust yourself to make wise decisions, better ones than in the past. Life is all about learning. Some lessons are easier than others. But all require you to have faith in how you've grown by making mistakes."

"I should've known better. Vince was a monster in disguise. From now on, how will I know it won't happen again?" Misty stared at the flowers and then froze. "Susie, I don't mean to insinuate that David is that kind of man, that I don't trust him."

"Of course not. How and if David fits into your life in this small town is up to you, as it should be." Susie squeezed her hand. "I know you've been hurt in the past. You can move forward from that, learn from that, trust yourself."

Misty smiled, realizing she had indeed learned from the past. David was a man who was always worthy of her trust. He'd shown her in so many ways. He'd been patient while she'd been working through her issues. And she knew he truly cared about her.

"Thank you, Susie. You've helped me realize what I should've recognized all along."

Susie stood and kissed Misty on the cheek. "Come talk to me anytime."

Misty watched her go, grateful for Susie's presence in her life.

CHAPTER TWENTY-THREE

AFTER A QUIET WEEKEND, MISTY WAS READY TO GET BACK to her kids at school. For the most part, they were an easy group. So far, all seemed eager to learn, and she intended to enjoy each day with them.

As she and Hazel walked into the school together, Hazel said, "I missed you this weekend. Maybe next one, we can do something together."

"That would be nice. I'm sorry I've neglected you. I just needed some time to myself."

They parted ways and went to their classrooms. Misty wanted to do more reading instruction with her students this week to see how and if she could set up a volunteer program for those who needed help.

After everyone had arrived, Misty noticed that both Brody and Violet were absent. She checked messages and saw that Violet was sick—nothing about Brody.

Trying to hide her worry, Misty began her day.

Mid-morning, Brody appeared with the school secretary.

"Brody was upset about being late and was afraid you'd be angry," explained the secretary.

"Oh, no. I'm so happy you're here," Misty said, smiling at

him. "You can go in and sit in your seat."

"We overslept," said Brody, handing her a check-in slip from the office.

"Well, I'm sure glad you came. I was missing you. Brody, you can work on math at Table 3 while those in the reading circle will continue to read with me."

Misty went over to Table 3, saw that Brody had the right paperwork, and returned to the circle, aware that Brody must not have had a bath. His fingernails were dirty, and he smelled.

When it came time for recess, Brody was hesitant to go outside. Misty realized that without Violet befriending him, he felt insecure.

"Better hurry, Brody!" she said. She saw that he was outside, and then she stood with her former schoolteacher, who was supervising recess.

"How's everything going?" Marilyn asked.

"Good," Misty replied. "I'm thinking of ways I can use volunteers to help my students who are behind in reading. Have you done something like that before?"

"Yes," said Marilyn.

"I haven't asked my student's parents yet. Most of them work."

"Why don't you start with the one?" Marilyn said.

"Okay, that's what I'll do," Misty said.

Marilyn indicated Brody. "Is this the student you were worried about?"

"I'm keeping an eye on him. Nolan warned me not to rush to judgment."

"It's a sensitive situation," Marilyn said, and Misty merely nodded.

After school, Misty sat outside on the deck of her cabin while Sugar ran and played in the woods, challenging a squirrel to come down from a tree branch to play with her.

Later, she went through her school papers and discovered her students were stronger at math than reading. Science was something she wanted to make full of fun lessons for them. Kids that age were so curious.

When David phoned that evening, she immediately picked up the call. "Hi, David. It's good to hear from you. I've been doing some writing exercises my therapist gave me."

"I'm glad," he said. "I've missed you."

"Me, too. Missed you, I mean. How are things going at work?"

They chatted about their jobs for a while, and Misty enjoyed their interaction. After their conversation ended, Misty smiled, grateful for David reaching out to her. It was a new beginning,

The next day, Brody appeared at school on time and had a bath. Violet was back and seemed to make Brody more comfortable. Misty silently blessed the little girl.

Misty spent time with each student for at least a few minutes, getting to know them better and determining their strengths and learning styles. A few, like Brody, needed to keep busy and were rewarded with reading, puzzles, or math games, while others needed more time to complete tasks. Some needed extra attention in reading and math.

She sent an email to Nolan letting him know she planned to get volunteers in her class.

He didn't object to the idea but let her know all volunteers needed training, citing privacy issues and how to address various problems.

"Thank you," Misty said, determined to follow through.

As luck would have it, Violet's mother, Alesha Allen, was the President of the PTA. After speaking to her on the phone, Misty was encouraged. They arranged to meet for coffee at the Lilac Lake Café Saturday afternoon.

On Friday, Hazel waited for Misty to gather her things. "It's been a while since we've been to Jake's. Want to go tonight?"

"I do," said Misty. "I need time to unwind."

"Great. I do too," Hazel said.

That evening, Misty headed to Jake's with Hazel, wondering who in their crowd would show up. Misty couldn't wait to see everyone and realized her time of wanting to be by herself was over. She had a stronger sense of who she was and how to react better to others.

As she and Hazel entered Jake's, she saw that Dani and Brad were already there, along with Sarah Bullard, Aaron Collister, Dirk, and Samantha. Others would show up as they could.

She slid into a chair next to Sarah. "How's the hardware store doing?"

"Okay. I have a little more time to help my parents now that my twins are in kindergarten. The girls also attend a playschool in the afternoons, and we all love it."

Aaron and Sarah exchanged smiles, and Misty realized something was going on between them. She caught Aaron's eye. He bobbed his head, inscrutable as always. She'd always admired his quiet ways, which was one reason he and David were friends.

She looked up as David entered the restaurant and felt herself warmed by his search for her. Seeing the empty chair beside her, David walked over and took it.

"Hi, Misty. Glad to see you," he said, reaching for her hand.

She smiled. "As we talked about last night, I'd like to continue where we left off."

"Me, too," said David. He laced his fingers through hers and squeezed.

She gazed into his face, loving the sight of him. She'd needed clarity and now knew he was exactly what she needed in her life. It might take time for their relationship to grow even deeper, but like a little seedling, she'd give it a chance to bloom.

More and more of their group arrived, increasing the noise and teasing among them. Misty was happy to feel part of the group again. Tomorrow, Crystal and Emmett would return home. Misty could hardly wait to see them.

JoEllen arrived and pulled up a chair to Misty's table.

"Where's Harley?" Sarah asked.

"He and I had a big fight. I found out he has a little boy when he mentioned that Misty was his teacher. I told him it was unfair to keep that to himself, that I'm not ready to be a mother."

JoEllen turned to Misty. "You should have told me. We're friends."

Misty shook her head. "I just teach his son in school. I had no idea you were dating his father until I saw you together. Frankly, it's none of my business."

"But you knew. And you had to know he was still married!!" JoEllen's face got bright red. "School records would show that." She burst into tears. "You've ruined everything. It's all your fault."

"I don't know how you can blame me," Misty said, horrified by the implications.

"Stop it, JoEllen," said David, coming to Misty's defense. "None of this is Misty's fault."

JoEllen got up and went into the bathroom.

Whitney and Nick arrived as JoEllen returned to the table, red-eyed.

After David explained the situation to Nick, Nick turned to

JoEllen and said firmly, "Misty is not to blame. If anyone is to blame, it's yourself."

JoEllen dabbed at her eyes and nodded.

After the conversation among the group slowed, Misty turned to David. "I'm going home. It's been a long week. I'm glad we had the opportunity to see one another tonight. I meant what I said. I hope we can continue our relationship."

"We can. How about letting me take you out tomorrow night for dinner?"

Misty smiled. "I'd like that."

"Let me walk you to your car. It looks like Hazel will be here a while longer."

"She told me earlier that Mike was going to take her home."

Misty and David left the restaurant and walked to Misty's car, which was parked behind the commercial strip.

David waited while she unlocked the door, and when she turned to face him, he asked quietly, "May I?"

Smiling, she lifted her face to his.

As his lips met hers, she let out a soft moan. This was what she wanted. This is what she needed.

When they pulled apart, David smoothed her hair away from her cheeks and stared at her. "I know it's early, and maybe you're not ready, but I'm falling in love with you. I have been for a long time. I'll be patient, but I need to know if you want this, too."

"Yes," she sighed happily.

"Then, that's what we'll do." He hugged her. "I'm good at

growing things, even relationships."

She chuckled. "I'm counting on that."

As Misty pulled into her driveway, she was still floating with happiness. David was the man she wanted in her life, now and in the future.

Her cell phone beeped, and thinking it might be him saying goodnight, she clicked on the text message: *"You're going to pay for your nosiness! I'll make sure of it!"*

All romantic thoughts fled as fear wove through her. She didn't recognize the number, but she was pretty sure it was from Harley. She surveyed the area around her and looked up as a truck sped away. The thought that it might've been Harley had her running to her front door and working fast with the alarm to get inside.

Sugar, excited as always to greet her, helped to steady her nerves as she let the dog outside and then quickly reset the alarm.

She got into her pajamas, and feeling a bit silly, she practiced some of the karate moves David had shown her.

The next morning, Misty awoke with a sense of anticipation. Crystal and Emmett were coming home from Paris, and later, she was going out with David. It was bound to be a nice, full day.

She snuggled with Sugar and then sat on the back deck

while Sugar spent time in the woods. Braver now, Sugar drank water from the creek and then went back to sniffing and exploring.

Sipping her coffee, Misty was content to sit and watch her.

Her cell phone rang. *Hazel.*

"Hi! Did you have fun last night?" Misty asked her.

"I did, but it's a good thing you left. JoEllen got into a big fight with Harley at Jake's. Harley was furious that JoEllen had dumped him, and he blamed you for interfering in his life. Dani and Brad convinced Harley to leave, and Mike dropped JoEllen off at her cabin before taking me home. I thought you'd want to know to stay clear of them both."

"Thanks for alerting me. The situation between them is a mess. I'm going to stay out of it. Now, what are you doing today?"

Mike and Ross are going into Portsmouth, and Melissa and I are going with them. We'll have lunch and look around while they take care of some business. How are things with David?

Misty felt her lips curve. "He and I have decided to grow our relationship."

Hazel chuckled. "Very appropriate. You two are great together."

"I'm happy that we're working on it," said Misty. "Thanks for the warning about Harley. I got a text message last night that I'm pretty sure came from him. So, believe me, I'm on the alert."

"Do you think you should mention it to Nick? As police

chief, he might want to know about it," said Hazel.

"Maybe later. Right now, I don't want to escalate it."

"I understand," said Hazel. "Guess I'd better go."

"Thanks for the call," said Misty. "Have a fun day!"

"You too," said Hazel, ending the conversation.

Misty set down her coffee cup and stared out at the water rushing in the creek below.

CHAPTER TWENTY-FOUR

THE NEXT AFTERNOON, MISTY WAS CLEANING EMMETT'S house, which his temporary replacement had left a mess. Her cell phone rang. She saw Crystal's number and picked up the call.

"*Bonjour*! Where are you?" Misty couldn't hide her excitement.

"We're just leaving Logan airport in Boston," said Crystal. "We'll be home in a couple of hours."

"That will give me time to finish up here," said Misty. "Emmett's replacement seems like a nice guy, but he's a slob. I don't want you coming home from your honeymoon to a dirty house."

"Oh, Misty, that's sweet of you," gushed Crystal.

"I'm happy to do it," Misty said. "Don't worry about fresh food. I took care of that earlier."

"You're an angel. It's been a fantastic trip, but I'll be happy to be home. And Emmett is ready to get back to his patients. Guess we're just a couple of homebodies."

Emmett mumbled something in the background, and Crystal laughed. "Maybe not. Emmett's reminding me of how I loved our time in Paris. Like I said, it was fabulous."

"Can't wait to hear all about it. See you shortly," said Misty, ending the call. She had more work to do.

Misty had just placed a vase filled with wildflowers on the kitchen table when she heard a car pulling into the driveway. She hurried outside to see Crystal get out of a Lincoln Town Car and rushed to greet her.

They hugged and laughed when they both tried to talk at the same time.

"I'm delighted to see you," said Misty, blinking back a sting of tears. Crystal was much more than a sister to her.

"And I to see you," Crystal said, holding Misty away from her and studying her. "You look different. Happier. Are you?"

"Yes, it's been a couple of difficult weeks, but I feel as if I'm on the right track now. Tell me all about the trip. Were the food and wine as wonderful as you thought?"

Crystal patted her stomach. "Even more so. I have many delicious ideas for gourmet dinners. But nothing can beat the fresh bread, cheese, and wine for a simple picnic. That, too, exceeded all my expectations."

"And the clothing?" Misty asked, noticing the scarf Crystal was wearing.

"The fabrics, the styles, the French flair are all wonderful. It felt nice to dress up every day. I'd gotten too used to wearing my cooking outfits."

Emmett came over to them and kissed Misty on the cheek. "Your sister caught the attention of everyone. Seems like I have a natural French woman on my hands."

Misty's heart lifted as Emmett smiled at Crystal as if she were the most beautiful woman in the world. Remembering David's kiss, she was pleased things were going well for her, too.

"Why don't you come to help me unpack?" Crystal said. "I bought a few items for you, and I'm anxious to see if you like them."

They went inside the house while Emmett walked over to the medical practice building to check on things there.

In the kitchen, Crystal turned to her. "It looks fantastic. Thanks for straightening and cleaning. I liked Emmett's replacement when I met him, but I had a feeling that the house would need sprucing up by the time we returned."

"It certainly did," said Misty, shuddering to think of how disappointed Crystal would have been to come home to such a mess.

They went upstairs to Crystal's bedroom. Crystal opened her suitcase to show Misty some of her purchases. They squealed excitedly as her sister unwrapped each one like a special Christmas package.

"And this is for you," said Crystal, handing her a small, soft package.

Misty opened it and gasped with pleasure. "I've read about Hermes scarves but never thought I'd own one. I love it!" She held up the red floral scarf and wrapped it around her neck.

Crystal kissed her. "In Paris, women wear scarves in a variety of ways. They add elegance to any outfit. I want you to enjoy this bit of luxury."

"Every time I wear it, I'll feel like a princess," said Misty, staring at herself with the scarf in the mirror.

"And one more thing." Crystal handed her another larger package. "You'll get a ton of wear out of this."

Misty unwrapped the tissue, stared at the simple, sleeveless, black sheath, and grinned. "My own little black dress. Thank you. Thank you."

"I enjoyed picking these out for you. Wear them with health and joy," said Crystal. "Now, I suppose I should do some laundry. How's that for a dramatic change?"

Misty laughed. "From riches to rags."

"Are you going to Jake's tonight?" Crystal asked.

"I'm not sure. David is taking me out to dinner."

Crystal smiled. "He's perfect for you."

"We've decided to let our relationship develop. I had a bit of a setback and needed to figure some things out, but I feel better about us now. I'll tell you about it another time. I know you're anxious to get unpacked and settled. I'm glad you had such a marvelous time."

"Me, too," said Crystal. "We'll talk tomorrow."

Misty carried her gifts to her car, overwhelmed by Crystal's generosity. She intended to put the dress to use by wearing it this evening, along with her scarf.

Misty spent the remainder of the afternoon anxiously

awaiting a call from David to confirm a time for dinner. She knew that as long as fair weather held, he'd be busy with the landscaping business. Today was no exception.

When he finally called to say he'd pick her up at seven, she laid her new black dress on her bed. It was cool enough to wear the scarf Crystal had given her. That, and simple gold earrings would make the outfit. Misty thought of the evening as a new beginning with David and wanted to look especially nice.

Later, when David picked her up, she was rewarded for her efforts by a long, low whistle from him.

"You look amazing," David said as he bent to kiss her.

She looked up at him and grinned. "Do I look Parisian?"

At his look of confusion, she laughed. "Crystal brought me the dress and scarf from Paris. I'm supposed to feel very special in them."

He gave her an impish look. "I think you'd look very special without any of it. We can give it a try later."

She chuckled as heat rose to her cheeks. Maybe this was more than a simple new beginning. The thought intrigued her.

They left the house, and David helped her get into his truck.

She hooked her seat belt and turned to him in the driver's seat. "Where are we going?"

"I thought we'd eat at Fresh. The owners have started construction on their new restaurant here in town, and I wanted a chance to taste their food at their other place."

"What a treat! I've eaten there once before. Though their menu is on the pricey side, their fresh selections are worth it."

"I thought it was the perfect spot for our first real date in a while," said David.

"Thanks," said Misty, noting his tan slacks and navy golf shirt. He'd fussed with his appearance, too.

When they arrived at the restaurant outside of town, a valet took care of David's truck while David led her inside.

As they waited to be seated, Misty studied the interior. Dark green walls were trimmed with white-painted wood and matched the green in the floral-patterned carpet. White linen cloths covered the tables, and in the center of each table, a small crystal vase held pink roses. The lighting was low, allowing the shimmering candles at each table to glow.

They were seated at a corner table where they'd have privacy.

"It's beautiful," said Misty.

David took hold of her hand and gazed at her, smiling with satisfaction. "I wanted this to be a special evening to celebrate our decision to move forward."

"That makes me happy," said Misty. David had never given her a reason to doubt his sincerity.

Their waitress appeared, and after ordering a bottle of wine, David and she perused the menu together.

"What do you think you want?" he asked her. He hesitated for only a moment, then added, "Along with me?"

She laughed. "That's dessert. Right? I think I'll start with something on the menu."

He chuckled. "This is a side of you I like."

They laughed together. She enjoyed flirting with him. It was something new for her.

The wine came, and David went through the motions of tasting it. "Delicious."

The wine steward bobbed his head. "A lovely Chandler Hill pinot noir. A fine choice."

After pouring some into their glasses, he left, giving them privacy.

David took a sip of wine and set down his glass. "I have something to ask you, and I don't want it to come out wrong. My parents have been given a chance to buy a condo in Florida, and they wanted to know how I felt about moving into the cottage from the cabin. They eventually want a smaller place here in town but hate the idea of giving up the lake property."

"And?" Misty said, trying to control her voice as her heart pumped blood through her.

"And I wonder if you'd consider living there with me if our relationship grows like we want. Don't get me wrong. I'm not pushing you into anything before it's time, but if it's a flat no, I should probably let them know I'm not interested."

"What timeline are you talking about?" Misty asked.

"No definite decision has to be made for a long time. But as I said, if I know that no matter what happens between us, you have no interest in living there, I need to tell them." He shook his head. "I'm afraid it's beginning to sound awkward, and I don't want that."

"Would I ever consider living there if the circumstances were right?" she asked. "I would. Does that help?"

"Yes," said David. "We've committed to growing our relationship. Right?"

Misty nodded but already knew she wanted more. A lot of her recent soul-searching had included such thoughts.

"I think I'd better have another sip of wine and shut up," David said, grinning. "This opportunity for my parents has made me think about the future."

"No worries. We're starting over tonight, and that was a fair question," said Misty. If they were going to grow and move forward, they had to be able to talk about anything.

They placed their orders, and Misty told him about working at the gourmet dinners Crystal was excited to put on. David spoke about the coming Christmas season and how he planned to increase sales.

"Maybe you could have a booth at the Christmas Fair in town," said Misty. "That might help you get through slow winter months."

"Something to think about, anything to be able to keep my crew. Seasonal work can make it hard for families. Several of my men work at the ski resorts during the winter, but anything I can do to help keeps a flow of income for everyone."

"You're a good man, David," she said.

"I try." He gave her a teasing smile. "But there are times I like to be bad."

Laughing, she shook her head but didn't respond.

Their meals were brought to the table.

She'd ordered a crispy chicken breast stuffed with mushrooms in a lemon-butter sauce. David, a typical male, asked for a strip steak. Both looked delicious. A mélange of fresh vegetables accompanied the entrées.

Misty took a bite of her chicken and sighed with pleasure. "Yum."

"Mine, too," said David. "If this restaurant is an indication, I think Refresh, the new restaurant in town, will do very well."

After a pleasant meal, they headed to Misty's house. The closer they got, the more anticipation grew inside Misty. She hoped that this evening would prove the depth of their commitment to one another. It was both scary and exciting to have reached this stage in their relationship.

Sugar greeted them with her usual excitement, and Misty took the opportunity to suggest they sit out on the deck while Sugar roamed in the woods.

"Can I get you something to drink? Water? Coffee?" she asked David.

"A glass of water would be nice," he replied. He stood at the deck railing and looked into the woods. "It's peaceful here. I love hearing the sound of the rushing river."

"Yes, it's very soothing," said Misty. She went inside, fixed two glasses of water, and returned to the deck with them.

She handed David a glass and sat in one of the chairs. "Thanks again for a wonderful dinner. It was delicious."

"I thought so too. More importantly, it was a chance for me to do something nice for you. I know you've had a rough beginning with your job at school."

"It has been a big learning curve for me. I know my responsibilities as a teacher and a person, but I have to be careful how I use them."

"Harley Kirk is a troubled man if he doesn't want to admit he has a son or that he's married. I don't think we've heard the end of him yet, even with JoEllen breaking up with him. After all, he works at The Meadows."

"I can't help wondering what is going on with him. There's got to be more to the story."

"It'll all work out the way it's meant to be," said David, sounding like his mother, making Misty smile.

His gaze remained fixed on her, and when Sugar came bounding back, Misty opted to go inside.

David followed her.

In the kitchen, they set down their glasses and faced one another.

"We teased about dessert earlier …"

"Yes," said Misty, both commenting and answering his unspoken question.

"Are you sure?" David asked her.

She took his hand and walked with him to her bedroom.

"Not now," she said to Sugar and closed the bedroom door.

David cupped her face in his strong hands, toughened by labor, and lowered his lips to hers. His kiss was sweet and soft until passion took over, and it grew hungry.

She responded and felt her knees weaken. His kisses told a unique story, one filled with both tenderness and passion, of caring and needing.

When they pulled apart, he murmured, "Wow," in such a way she knew he felt the same awe.

Emboldened, aware of the importance of taking the next step, she moved toward the bed, draping her scarf across a chair in the bedroom.

He came up behind her and nuzzled her neck. "M-m-m, you smell good."

She turned and faced him, wanting him to see how much she needed him.

He drew her to him and unzipped the back of her dress. She stepped out of it and draped it on top of her scarf.

David lifted her into his arms and carried her to the bed, gently laying her on top of it. "This is what I've waited for. I want you so much. Do you feel the same?"

"Yes, oh yes." She opened her arms to him, and he fell into them.

CHAPTER TWENTY-FIVE

THE NEXT MORNING, MISTY AWOKE, THRILLED TO SEE David sleeping beside her. At the bottom of the bed, Sugar eyed her with a knowing look from the blanket Misty had placed there for her. She and David had needed privacy, but after they'd made delicious love, Sugar wanted her nightly sleep on the bed—a fair compromise.

Misty patted the space next to her, and Sugar crawled up and spooned beside her. Behind them, David stirred and reached for Misty.

Sugar leaped over Misty and snuggled with David.

"Guess that's good as a sign that Sugar approves of you," said Misty, rolling over and patting David's stubbled cheek.

"Morning," said David, lifting her hand and kissing it.

She loved how, even now, he was both passionate and gentle.

"Why don't I fix coffee for the two of us and take care of Sugar?" she asked him.

"Great. If you don't mind, I'll grab a quick shower, and then I'll be ready for the day. My treat for breakfast at the café."

"Deal," she said.

Misty wrapped a robe around herself and padded into the

kitchen to let Sugar out. She made a pot of coffee and decided to take a cup to David.

He was in the bathroom drying off when she handed him the coffee. "Ah, just what I need. Thanks."

"I'm going to take a shower, and then I'll be ready to go to the café," she said.

"No problem," said David. "I'll help." He set down the coffee cup. "I'll wash ... your back ... or whatever."

She laughed. Their lovemaking last night had been filled with joy. And by the look of it, it was going to move forward that way. She was thrilled she'd taken a chance on him, on herself.

At the café, Emmett and Crystal were sitting at a table outside with a crowd gathered around them.

Misty waved at Crystal, and Crystal motioned her forward. "Come sit with us. We've hardly been able to eat with everyone greeting us. You two sitting here might make it seem as if we're too busy to answer a lot of questions."

"I'm sure everyone wants to know how your trip to Paris went," said Misty.

Crystal pulled on the shoulders of her T-shirt. "See? *J'aime Paris*. That should be a sign of how much I liked it."

"Yes, but people are still curious. I have lots of questions about it myself."

Emmett and David shook hands, and after David had taken

a seat in a chair next to him, the two men began to converse.

Crystal nudged Misty. "Is this, the two of you together, what I think it is?"

Misty's smile was an answer of its own. "David and I are taking our relationship seriously. I haven't told him, but I love him."

"And David?" Crystal asked quietly.

"Before last night, he said he was falling in love with me," whispered Misty.

"Hey, you two? Ready to order? I see a waitress heading our way," said Emmett.

The four of them ordered, and Misty listened as Crystal told them about her favorite parts of Paris.

After their meal was finished, Misty and David left.

"It's a nice day. Want to go to the cottage? I need to check on my family's little fishing boat there."

"Sure. It'll be fun as long as I can bring Sugar. I'm forced to leave her alone during the week. I don't want to leave her alone too much over the weekends."

"That seems fair, and you know my family and I love her."

When they went back to her cabin to pick up Sugar, Misty decided to follow David in her car to save him a trip back to town.

Sugar seemed to know an adventure was in store for her and eagerly jumped into the back seat.

Misty and David headed out together.

As she drove, Misty's mind flooded with sweet memories of last night. David had been gentle with her. Even as their passion rose, he'd sensed her moment of panic at being beneath him and eased away for a moment until the feeling passed. She'd never experienced that consideration and realized how lucky she was to find someone so strong and yet so caring.

When she pulled into the cottage's driveway, Sugar rushed to the door, yipping with excitement. Misty let the dog out and stood a moment studying the cottage. The idea of living there someday made her view it in a whole new way. It was a lovely home, a great place for animals and children. But she'd want to put her mark on it, change things in the interior.

David walked over to her. "What do you think?"

"It's a beautiful spot," she said, unwilling to say more. Neither of them was ready for a major commitment beyond the one they'd made. But the idea that the possibility was there filled Misty with anticipation.

Susie came out of the house and walked toward them.

"You're in time. I've just pulled carrot cake muffins from the oven. Come on in."

Misty laughed at the grin on David's face. She knew that carrot cake was his favorite.

As they walked into the house, Susie put an arm around Misty. "I have some news to share with you. It's about Brody."

"I hope it's good news," said Misty.

"I'd say it's encouraging," Susie said. "Can I get you coffee, lemonade, or something else to go with a muffin?"

"I'd love a glass of lemonade, and I certainly won't say no to a muffin," said Misty.

Susie served them all drinks and muffins and suggested to Misty that they sit in the sunroom to talk.

Seated there, the two of them faced one another. "I know how concerned you've been about Brody Kirk. I've learned that though the parents have been separated for a while, the family moved here recently to be with Brody's grandparents. I met his grandmother at church this morning. She told me her daughter had been away in an addiction recovery program and that while she was gone, Brody's father had insisted on raising him alone. Brody's mother is better and now is able to take care of Brody with the grandmother's help."

"What about Brody's father?" Misty asked.

"I'm not sure. Brody and his mother are staying with her parents."

"Are Brody's parents going to get back together?" asked Misty.

"I don't know. It wasn't mentioned," said Susie. "But the grandmother did say that they have you to thank for the changes. A teacher at your school mentioned your concern for Brody to her."

"I'm glad I could help, but I hope it won't be seen as meddling by Harley. He was very angry at me for speaking out about Brody's welfare. He still is."

"Some changes are in store for him, but if Harley really loves his son, he'll go along with them," said Susie. "Time will tell. How is your volunteer program going?"

"I haven't approached many of the parents yet because most of them work." Misty smiled at her. "But you've given me an idea. Would the older women at your church be willing to volunteer?"

"I bet some would. I can ask around for you."

Misty set down her plate and gave Susie a hug. "That would be fantastic."

As they hugged one another, Misty realized what a blessing it was that, in addition to loving David, she'd found a family with him.

"C'mon. Let's take a cruise around the lake," David said.

The boat's engine was small, low in power, and quiet. Large boats with powerful, noisy engines were not allowed on the lake, which made it pleasant for everyone.

As they followed the shoreline in the boat, Misty had a view of the land and houses. The Lilac Lake Inn looked as natural as the smaller dwellings as it nestled against the woods behind it.

Sugar stood at the bow of the boat, facing the slight wind as the boat slowly chugged along.

"Sugar sure loves it here," said David.

"We both do," said Misty, feeling a part of the family.

###

After having a simple but delicious chicken dinner at his parent's house, David walked Misty and Sugar to her car.

"I'll call you this week, and we can meet at Jake's. It's a busy time for both of us." He leaned down and kissed her. His lips were soft but sure, letting her know how much he cared. "I'll miss you."

"Me, too," she said, meaning it in a way she'd never felt.

He kissed her again, and when they finally pulled apart, they smiled at one another, content.

Misty put Sugar into the car and climbed behind the wheel, sorry the weekend was ending.

At home, Misty pulled into her driveway and sighed. The cabin would seem quiet and empty without David.

Startled, she heard a truck pulling up behind her, so close it almost rammed her car.

Misty got out and faced Harley. Her pulse sprinted. "What do you want?"

Anger made his face frightening.

Misty told herself to be calm and headed for the front door, aware she could push a security panic button there.

Harley caught her by the shoulder and jerked her to a stop.

"I thought I told you to mind your own business. Because of you, my wife is here, taking Brody away from me and telling me I have to get help."

"Are you talking about help for addiction?" Misty asked as old memories surfaced.

Harley came closer.

Misty could see the glazed look in his eyes and smelled alcohol on his breath. She stepped back.

"You bitch! Don't look at me like that. None of this is your fucking business," he snarled and lunged for her.

Misty's mind went into overdrive. She raised a hand, kicked out with one leg, and then slammed a hand down on his neck, karate style.

Harley tumbled to the ground and lay there, looking up at her wide-eyed. He tried to scramble to his feet and fell back.

Misty stood, poised to strike again. Exhilaration filled her. She'd never felt this strong, so unafraid. In her mind, she knew if she ever had to face Vince again, she could do it.

Keeping watch over Harley, Misty punched in Nick's number and asked him to send someone over to take care of Harley, who lay sprawled on the ground.

A few minutes later, Nick arrived in his police car and hurried over to her. "Are you okay?" He glanced at Harley on the ground.

"I had to do a few karate moves on him, but I'm fine," said Misty. "David's lessons and my practice paid off."

Nick clapped her on the back. "Good job. We'll put him in jail and let him sober up."

"Thanks." She realized Sugar was still in the car and let her out. Her friendly, sweet dog growled at Harley as he was taken to the police car, and then Sugar ran back to her.

Trembling now, Misty picked up Sugar and hugged her.

Later, giving David the news, she said, "It was as if a gray cloud blocked out anything else and I remembered all the moves you showed me. And best of all, I finally feel free from the past. I have you to thank in more ways than one."

"You deserve it," said David. "I love you, you know."

"And I love you, David," she said, delighted to be able to tell him at last.

"I'm coming over."

CHAPTER TWENTY-SIX

THE NEXT MORNING, MISTY STOOD INSIDE HER CLASSROOM, anxiously anticipating the arrival of her students. She could hardly wait to see Brody.

Even before he reached the door, she could see a difference in the way he walked, with more confidence than usual. It looked as if he was wearing a new shirt and pants, and his hair was combed.

When he saw her, he came forward to hand her a note. He stood by as she opened it and read:

Dear Ms. Owens,

I want to thank you for caring so much about my Brody. I'm told your concern for him at school helped get my family involved in making better changes for him. I'm back home now, and Harley, Brody's father, has agreed to get some help so he can stay in contact with his son.

Sincerely,

Karen Kirk

"Thank you," Misty said to Brody.

Brody looked up at her and studied her with big brown eyes. Then, after pausing a moment, he quickly hugged her and hurried away.

Misty's vision blurred. She'd do anything to help keep a child safe. This was proof of her efforts.

Later, when Nolan called her to his office, all she cared about was having Brody safe and loved.

Nolan greeted her at the door. Instead of asking her to take a seat, he closed the door behind her and stood facing her. "I heard from Brody's mother, and though I certainly don't approve of you getting overly involved in a student's family, I'm pleased Brody's family is making some changes, and Brody is staying at this school."

Misty stared at the floor, remembering how Susie had told her to take a deep breath and quietly state your position. "Are you okay?" Nolan asked. "I must ask if you're going to be comfortable having Brody in class after his father attacked you."

Surprised that he'd asked, Misty said, "Definitely. I really believe Brody's place is in my class."

"Okay. That will be all," said Nolan.

Misty studied him. After listening to him sound so self-important and noting his thin, lank figure, she was pretty sure she could take him down.

A slight smile lifted her lips.

Tuesday night, sitting with her friends at Jake's, Misty fielded their questions about how she'd handled Harley. As can happen in a small town, the more people heard about it, the more exaggerated the story became.

"All I can tell you is that karate lessons helped me. I still practice them at home as part of my exercise routine." She smiled at David. "I've got the best tutor around."

"I think we should all sign up for some classes with David," said Hazel.

"While we wouldn't want to intrude on Kung Fu Karate's business, a defensive class at our sports center might be a smart idea," said Ross. "I'll bring it to Mike's attention when he returns to town."

The conversation moved to other things, and Misty leaned back in her chair, content to let others talk. She liked simply being there.

When David called on Friday afternoon to ask her to meet him at the family garden to help with a special project for his mother, she was eager to comply. They had planned the whole weekend together.

Misty hooked Sugar to her leash and headed out the door.

The weather was lovely this afternoon in September, and Misty was delighted to be able to do something for Susie. She was a wonderful mother to David, and Misty felt as if Susie was becoming a mother to her.

Sugar trotted happily beside Misty as they made the familiar walk through town. Though the colors of Fall were beginning to appear, she knew that come May, the entire town would be showing off the beautiful purple colors of lilacs.

Misty waved to a neighbor and marveled at how comfortable she felt in Lilac Lake. Her fears from the past had been put in their proper place, and she was ready to move forward with her life, freer and happier than she'd ever been. The song of a cardinal trilled above her, and she stopped and looked up at the red bird, her favorite.

When they arrived at the garden, David waved at her from a back corner and motioned her forward.

"Hi, I'm here to help. What do you need me to do?" she asked, approaching him.

David held up a small rose plant. "My mother wants this garden to be important for all family members. She's asked me to plant this one here, by your favorite spot. I thought you might like to help me. It's for you."

Tears blurred Misty's vision. She realized this was Susie's way of welcoming her into the family. To be part of such a warm, loving one was a gift she'd always treasure. She fought for self-control.

"How sweet," she said, kneeling beside him.

David had already dug a hole. Together, they lowered the small plant into it, handling it carefully.

"It's such a beautiful pink color," said Misty, patting the earth gently around the plant, thinking about the honor that had been given.

"It's perfect," agreed David.

Still on their knees, they faced one another.

"I know it may seem soon, but my feelings for you have been growing for a long time. I knew I had to be patient, give you a chance to strengthen your roots, and become strong enough on your own to blossom. But I can't wait any longer. My love for you is like one of these beautiful blooms, ready to share with everyone. I need you. I love you. Will you marry me?"

Misty looked at him through fresh tears. She knew her life with David would be filled with the gentleness and care he gave all his seedlings, and like the one they'd just planted together, it would be healthy and beautiful.

David gazed at her with a loving expression and took hold of her hands. "Will you?"

"Yes, oh yes, David.   I'll marry you."

They held onto each other, and then David lifted her face to his. And with his kiss, she knew that true love was like a bloom opening to life. And now she was ready.

# # # # #

Thank you for reading *Love's Bloom*. If you enjoyed this book, please help other readers discover it by leaving a review on Amazon, Goodreads, BookBub, or your favorite site. It's such a nice thing to do.

Sign up for my newsletter and get a free story. I keep my newsletters short and fun with giveaways, recipes, and the latest must-have news about me and my books. Welcome! Here's the link:

https://BookHip.com/RRGJKGN

About the Author

A *USA Today* Best-Selling Author, Judith Keim is a hybrid author who both has a publisher and self-publishes. Ms. Keim writes heart-warming novels about women who face unexpected challenges, meet them with strength, and find love and happiness along the way. Her best-selling books are based, in part, on many of the places she's lived or visited and on the interesting people she's met, creating believable characters and realistic settings her many loyal readers love. Ms. Keim loves to hear from her readers and appreciates their enthusiasm for her stories.

Ms. Keim enjoyed her childhood and young-adult years in Elmira, New York, and now makes her home in Boise, Idaho, with her husband, Peter, and their lovable miniature Dachshund, Wally, and other members of her family.

While growing up, she was drawn to the idea of writing stories from a young age. Books were always present, being read, ready to go back to the library, or about to be discovered. All in her family shared information from the books in general conversation, giving them a wealth of knowledge and vivid imaginations.

"If you have enjoyed this book, please help other readers discover it by leaving a review on Amazon, Goodreads, Bookbub, or the site of your choice. And please check out my other books and series:"

The Hartwell Women Series

The Beach House Hotel Series

Fat Fridays Group

The Salty Key Inn Series

The Chandler Hill Inn Series

Seashell Cottage Books

The Desert Sage Inn Series

Soul Sisters at Cedar Mountain Lodge

The Sanderling Cove Inn Series

The Lilac Lake Inn Series

The Lilac Lake Books

"ALL THE BOOKS ARE NOW AVAILABLE IN AUDIO on Audible, iTunes, Findaway, Kobo and Google Play! So fun to have these characters come alive!"

Ms. Keim can be reached at **www.judithkeim.com**

To like her author page on Facebook and keep up with the news, go to: **http://bit.ly/2pZWDgA**

To receive notices about new books, follow her on Book Bub:

https://www.bookbub.com/authors/judith-keim

And here's a link to where you can sign up for her periodic newsletter! **http://bit.ly/2OQsb7s**

She is also on Twitter @judithkeim, LinkedIn, and Goodreads. Come say hello!

Acknowledgments

As always, I am eternally grateful to my team of editors, Peter Keim and Lynn Mapp, my book cover designer, Lou Harper, and my narrator for Audible and iTunes, Angela Dawe. They are the people who take what I've written and help turn it into the book I proudly present to you, my readers! I also wish to thank my coffee group of writers who listen and encourage me to keep on going. Thank you, Peggy Staggs, Lynn Mapp, Cate Cobb, Nikki Jean Triska, Joanne Pence, Melanie Olsen, and Megan Bryce. And to you, my fabulous readers, I thank you for your continued support and encouragement. Without you, this book would not exist. You are the wind beneath my wings.

www.ingramcontent.com/pod-product-compliance
Lightning Source LLC
Chambersburg PA
CBHW021042310726
48969CB00006B/1779